23
SUGAR CREEK GANG
The KILLER CAT

Paul Hutchens

MOODY PRESS
CHICAGO

Original Title: *We Killed a Wildcat at Sugar Creek*

ISBN: 0-8024-7027-0

5 7 9 10 8 6 4

Printed in the United States of America

PREFACE

Hi—from a member of the Sugar Creek Gang!

It's just that I don't know which one I am. When I was good, I was Little Jim. When I did bad things—well, sometimes I was Bill Collins or even mischievous Poetry.

You see, I am the daughter of Paul Hutchens, and I spent many an hour listening to him read his manuscript as far as he had written it that particular day. I went along to the north woods of Minnesota, to Colorado, and to the various other places he would go to find something different for the Gang to do.

Now the years have passed—more than fifty, actually. My father is in heaven, but the Gang goes on. All thirty-six books are still in print and now are being updated for today's readers with input from my five children, who also span the decades from the '50s to the '70s.

The real Sugar Creek is in Indiana, and my father and his six brothers were the original Gang. But the idea of the books and their ministry were and are the Lord's. It is He who keeps the Gang going.

PAULINE HUTCHENS WILSON

1

The first time anybody around Sugar Creek knew for sure there was a bloodthirsty, savage-tempered wildcat in the territory was when one of them sneaked into Harm Groenwald's pasture and killed three of his prize lambs.

I never will forget the hair-raising chills that ran up and down my spine the morning I heard about it.

We had just finished breakfast at our house when we got the news. It had been one of the most peaceful breakfasts we had had in a long time. Charlotte Ann, my mischievous-minded, usually-hard-to-manage baby sister had been being especially well behaved, not fussing or whining but behaving like most babies don't in the morning.

My grayish-brown-haired mother was sipping her coffee quietly and had a very contented look on her face as we all waited for my bushy-eyebrowed father to finish reading the Bible story he had just started.

As I listened, I didn't have any idea that part of what he was reading was going to get mixed up in the excitement of a wildcat hunt before the summer would pass.

The short Bible story was about a grown-up boy named Jacob, who had had a quarrel with his brother, Esau. To save his life he left home to go to another country where his mother used to live.

The first night of the long journey was spent in very rocky territory with steep cliffs and outcrops and different-shaped boulders piled on each other. It made me think of the rocky hills above Old Man Paddler's cabin. In fact, the hills in that part of Sugar Creek territory were not far from the haunted house we all knew about, and they were the best place in the world for wildcats to live and hunt and raise their families. Of course, I didn't think of that while Mom was sipping her coffee and Charlotte Ann was playing with her cute, pink, bare toes and Dad was reading along in his deep, gruff voice.

Anyway, while Jacob slept outdoors that night—using a stone for a pillow—he had a dream about a stairway leading all the way up to heaven. In the dream he saw angels going up and down on it.

In a minute Dad would finish reading, and then we'd have what Mom calls a Quaker prayer meeting. That means we'd all be quiet a minute and each one would think his own prayer to God just before Dad or Mom or maybe I would pray with out-loud words, and our day would be started right.

Then is when, all of a sudden, the phone started ringing in our front room.

I listened to see whether it was going to be our ring or somebody else's. I knew all the gang's numbers by heart: two longs and a short for Little Jim; two shorts and a long for Poetry; three shorts for Circus; two shorts for Big Jim; four shorts for Dragonfly; and ours was one long and one short.

Different other neighbors had different other numbers.

On our phone system, all anybody on our seven-phone line had to do if he wanted to talk to any other family on the line was to go to the phone, lift the receiver, and ring whatever number he wanted.

Of course, everybody on the party line could hear the phone ring in their own house and would know who was being called but not who was calling—unless they lifted their own receiver and did what is called "eavesdropping." Nobody was supposed to do that, but different people sometimes did and made different people mad at each other.

There was also a special ring, which was hardly ever used. It was called an "emergency ring," and nobody was supposed to ring it unless there was an actual emergency, such as an accident or a death in the family or somebody's cow had run away and couldn't be found. That emergency ring was two extra long longs and two very short shorts.

Well, our heads were all bowed at our breakfast table, and in my imagination I was up in the hills not far from the haunted house, lying on a stone pillow and watching angels moving up and down a golden stairway, sort of like people riding up and down on an escalator in a department store. And that was when I heard the jangling of the telephone. My mind was jarred all the way back to our kitchen table, and I was hearing the extralong ring, followed by another just-as-long long and then two short, sharp shorts.

"Emergency!" Mom, sitting beside Charlotte Ann's high chair, exclaimed, jumping like a scared rabbit that had been shot at and missed. A startled look came over her face, and she was out of her chair in a flurry, accidentally knocking over her chair to get across the kitchen floor as fast as she could, into the living room and to the phone to answer it.

All that excitement brought Charlotte Ann to baby-style life. Her arms flew out and up in several directions. She knocked over her blue mug of white milk, which spilled over the edge of her tray and splashed onto the floor. Mixy, our black-and-white house cat came from her box of straw by the kitchen stove and started lapping up as much of the spilled milk as she could before anybody in the family could mop it up and it'd be wasted.

In the living room Mom's voice gasped, "What! A wildcat! Who said so? How do you know?"

I was out of my chair even faster than Mom had gotten out of hers. I stood beside her at the phone, straining my ears to hear whoever's voice was on the other end of the line, but I couldn't. That is, I couldn't hear any *one* voice.

Instead, because Mom had her receiver about an inch from her ear, I heard a jumble of what sounded like a dozen women's voices. Everybody was talking to everybody, and almost nobody was listening to anybody.

I tell you there was a lot of excitement around our house after Mom hung up and explained what the emergency was. It was Harm Groenwald's fast-talking wife who had rung the emergency number. They'd had three of their prize lambs killed last night. Their carcasses had been torn in the same way that two of their other lambs had been a year ago.

"This time I'm going to find out what killed them!" Harm had told his wife. "I'm going to call Chuck Hammer."

Mrs. Groenwald said the Sugar Creek veterinarian had hurried out from town to have a look at the dead lambs. He used to live out West and had seen kills like that before. He turned the bodies over a few times and said grimly, "We've got either a mountain lion or a monster wildcat on our hands. They both kill the same way. See here?"

He showed Harm what he meant. "They always crush the neck bones in front of the shoulders, then tear into the carcass *behind* the shoulders and eat the heart and liver first."

"But whoever heard of a mountain lion or a wildcat around here?" Harm objected. "They don't live in this part of the country!"

"*One* does," Chuck said, "and he's a big one! Huge!"

They found its tracks in a muddy place, and Chuck said, "Wildcat! I'd say thirty-five pounds, anyway. Maybe forty-five!"

Harm Groenwald's fast-talking, high-pitched-voiced wife told all that to all the people who had answered the emergency ring—told it in less than a minute and a half. It took Mom almost three minutes to tell it to Dad and me.

Dad quick got on the phone then and asked the vet, who was still at Groenwald's house, to stop at our farm on his way back to town. Addie, our red mother hog, had given us a litter of six pigs last night, and Dad thought Chuck ought to look her over and maybe suggest a better diet for her so that her babies would grow stronger fast.

I helped Mom clean up Charlotte Ann's spilled milk and finished just in time to go out to the hog lot where Dad and the veterinarian were talking about the monster of a wildcat and also where Chuck was giving Addie a physical checkup.

"She's all right," he told Dad. "She's given you six of the healthiest pigs I've ever seen. Not a runt in the litter."

Poetry, my best friend, had heard the emergency ring and was on the way to our house to talk it over with me when he'd hitched a ride with Chuck. So he was there, too. That was one reason I didn't quite finish helping Mom clean up the kitchen. I needed to get out where all the excitement was.

Standing by Addie's gate, Poetry started a singsongy little ditty he'd learned somewhere:

"Six little pigs in the straw with their
    mother,
  Bright eyes, curly tails, tumbling on
    each other;
  Bring them apples from the orchard
    trees,
  And hear those piggies say, 'Please,
    please, please.'"

I told Poetry it was a cute rhyme, and that started him off in a singsong again.

In fact, right that minute there was a glad singsong feeling in my mind. There had been ever since Harm Groenwald's wife had told Mom and Mom had told Dad and me that it was a wildcat that had killed Harm's two lambs last year as well as this year's three. It had been a wildcat and not a *dog* that had done it!

You know why I was glad if you've read the story *The Bull Fighter*. I never will forget those 10,000 minutes—which is how many minutes it took for a week to pass. Wally, my city cousin, had spent the whole 10,000 minutes at our farm. And Alexander the Coppersmith, his ill-mannered, city-bred dog, had been with him, the most uncontrollable dog there ever was.

Anyway, the night Harm Groenwald's two lambs were killed was the same night Wally's nervous mongrel had unleashed himself. It was my fault that his collar was too loose. *My fault*, I had thought again and again, *that two innocent lambs had been killed!*

I hadn't told anybody. One reason was that, if they ever proved it was Wally's dog that had done it, then Alexander would have to be shot, and I'd be to blame for *his* death, too. It'd be a shame for a city dog that didn't know any better to have to lose his life.

So I'd put off telling anybody, but I shouldn't have. I should have told what Alexander did before Wally took his dog home to Memory City with him.

But now I'd never have to! Feeling glad in my heart toward God for making everything work out the way it had, and because I was in the habit of talking out loud to Him anytime I felt like it, I all of a sudden said, "Thanks! Thanks a lot!"

Poetry, not knowing what I'd been thinking, answered with his squawky, ducklike voice, "I'm glad you like it. I'll sing it again." And he was off in another half-bass singsong about the six little pigs in the straw with their mother.

We were all interrupted then by the sound of dogs' voices coming from the direction of Harm Groenwald's pasture. I'd heard those same long-voiced hounds before. My mind's eye told me it was Jay and Bawler, Circus Browne's dad's big coonhounds. I was sure they were on the trail of the wildcat. Already Harm Groenwald had called on the best hunter with the best hounds in the whole territory to help him catch the wild beast that had killed his sheep.

Many a time at night I'd heard those dog voices hot on a coon trail along the bayou or the swamp or in the rocky hill country above Old Man Paddler's Lincoln-style cabin.

Jay is a big, long-bodied, hundred-pound bluetick with a deep, hollow bawl. Bawler is a lanky black-and-tan only about half as big as Jay. She has a high-pitched wail that sends chills up and down your spine when she's excited and going strong on a trail.

"Let's go join the hunt!" Poetry exclaimed.

And I answered, "Sure! Let's go."

Dad stopped us, though, by saying, "No, it's an organized hunt. The men have guns, and they won't want any boys along."

It didn't feel good to be stopped, but we weren't the only boys who didn't get to go. Circus, the best athlete and the acrobat of our gang, Dan Browne's only son, didn't get to go, either.

In a few minutes, there he was, coming through the orchard toward us. On a leash, running all around him in a lot of excitement, was his new hound pup he had named "Ichabod," one of the cutest black-and-tans you ever saw.

"The hounds are coming this way," Poetry cried. "Listen! That means Old Stubtail came this direction last night after he killed the lambs. I'll bet he's got his home down in the swamp or maybe along the bayou!"

"Or in the cave," a voice behind us piped up. It was Little Jim, the smallest member of the gang, who had come without making any noise.

Old Bawler and Jay were *really* coming our way. Already they were in the lane at the south side of our pasture—over the fence, through the pasture and watermelon patch, and straight for the pignut trees at the north end of our garden.

That was enough to scare me. It meant that last night after Old Stubtail, as Circus called him, had had his lamb dinner at Groenwalds', he had come across *our* south pasture, through *our* farmyard, and had been only a hundred yards from *our* henhouse and—

I got my thoughts interrupted then by the hound pup on Circus's leash going simply wild with excitement because Bawler was his mother, and he wanted to get into the excitement, whatever it was.

The pup was at the end of his leash, pulling and tugging and struggling wildly. And then his collar was over his head, and he was off toward the pignut trees to join in whatever kind of dog game his mother and old Jay were playing.

And that's when I heard the pup's hunting voice for the first time. It was a high-pitched, wailing tremolo, like the highest tone on the organ at our church. It was also the longest wail I'd ever heard.

Now there were *three* hounds, and I never saw hunting dogs more excited. They were as excited as if it had been only a few minutes since the big cat had gone through our orchard. They were over in the orchard now, heading through it toward Poetry's dad's woods and the mouth of the branch beyond and the cave beyond that and Old Man Paddler's hills beyond that.

Mr. Browne let out a yell when little Ichabod joined the chase. He ordered him to stop, but Ichabod wouldn't. It was too much fun. He was also using his own sense of smell to tell him where to trail.

At the orchard fence, though, the pup scared up a rabbit and went off in a different direction, giving chase with an even more excited voice than before.

Bawler and Jay were over the orchard fence and on their way toward the Sugar Creek bridge, and Ichabod was heading toward the place where he'd last seen the rabbit, which was near the beehives in the orchard.

Circus made a dive for his hound when he circled near, grabbed him, and soon had him on leash again. He also gave him a good scolding, saying, "Don't you *ever* do that again! *Never* leave one trail for another. Do you hear?"

Well, it was a long, hard chase for Dan Browne and his hounds. Finally, somewhere in the hills in dry, ragged outcrops above Old Man Paddler's cabin, the dogs lost the scent, and the hunt was over.

Thinking maybe Old Stubtail might come back to finish eating one of the lambs he'd killed, Circus's pop set a number three doublespring steel trap at a place in the fence where it was easy for a large cat to get through. He tied a feather on a string and hung it on an elderberry bush close to the trap so that the wind would blow it. The cat, belonging to the same family as a house cat, which would be attracted to anything like that, might see the feather, smell the bait near the trap, and get caught.

That night a farmer three miles down the creek lost a calf. The kill was the same kind—a broken neck in front of the shoulders, a hole behind the shoulder, and the heart and liver eaten out.

2

Dan Browne tried the dogs again, and again they lost the trail in the hills above Old Man Paddler's cabin. He tried setting traps in everyplace that looked like good cat cover, but always it was no use. Old Stubtail was too smart to let himself get caught.

Then for a week there were no more kills—not even one—and it began to look as if the big cat had moved to safer territory, maybe clear out of the county.

Two more weeks passed, and still nobody reported any livestock being killed. We all began to breathe more easily. Dan Browne felt sure the cat was gone, especially when Harm Groenwald reported that some wild animal had eaten a batch of special cat poison he'd put out in a likely place. After that, the reports of raiding stopped altogether.

Then the Sugar Creek county fair week came, and most of us got to go for a day. It was always fun to go where there were so many people and so many exhibits to see. Some of the gang won prizes for their lambs or pigs or calves.

It was while we were watching an acrobat doing stunts on a flying trapeze that Little Jim got the idea that *he* wanted to be a trapeze artist. There was almost no living with him for a while. He'd talk it, sing it, pretend it, and also act out all kinds of dangerous acrobatic stunts when he was with us.

Once, he leaped up, caught hold of the two-by-four at the east end of our grape arbor, swung his feet up and over, and "skinned the cat." Before I could stop him, he'd stood up and actually walked across from one end to the other.

"You're getting reckless," I told him. "You better not ever do that again!"

"Better stick to piano playing," Poetry told him.

As you know, Little Jim was the best boy pianist in the whole Sugar Creek territory. His mother was the organist and pianist in our church.

"My fingers get enough exercise," Little Jim said. "More than enough. I'm going to be an athlete all over."

And we couldn't stop him. He taught himself to do the cartwheel, shinny up trees faster than anything, and chin himself fifteen times. In our haymow he climbed high above the hay and walked across the highest beam, a proud grin on his face. I'd walked that beam myself a few times, and with the hay below it wasn't too dangerous. But it seemed ten times worse for Little Jim to do it.

But Little Jim was good and getting better. The only thing was, we didn't dare tell him *not* to climb up to any dangerous place, or he'd be sure to want to do it.

It was while he was still working hard learning to become a stunt man that we read a story in the *Sugar Creek Times* about sheep killings, lost calves, and even a colt killing in Parke County, almost a hundred miles from where we lived. And that, we decided, explained what had happened to Old Stubtail. He'd left our neighborhood for safer territory.

Because Mr. Browne's hounds were known all over the state and because he'd had better success than most anybody else running down "cats," as he called them, he got a phone call to bring Jay and Bawler and his traps to Parke County. Not only would he get a bounty for killing Old Stubtail, but the farmers would also make up a special purse of one hundred dollars for him.

Circus's pop, as you maybe know, used to be an alcoholic. But he wasn't anymore. He had turned his life over to God to let Him run it, and whiskey and beer and such had gone out.

I never will forget what I once heard him say. He was telling Little Tom Till's unbelieving, drinking father what had happened to him. They were standing at the spring down near the creek at the time. Dan Browne had just handed Old John Till a drink of water, and Old John said, "No thanks, I like this better." And he pulled a flask of whiskey from his hip pocket, lifted it to his lips, and took a swig.

Dan raised his voice and said sternly, "I *used* to do that, but when I let Christ into my life, alcohol went out for good. I was like old Bawler while I was training her to be a good coonhound. She kept getting after rabbits, possums, skunks—anything except what I wanted her to trail. I finally got her trained except for one thing. She'd always turn aside when she crossed a skunk track. I had to punish her again and again for that.

"Well, God had to punish *me* too—plenty. But He finally won. Now, every time I'm tempted to leave *His* trail for me, to chase off after something He doesn't want, I think of old Bawler and her polecat chasing." Mr. Browne took another sip of water from the spring. "Liquor is the worst skunk of all."

I saw hook-nosed John Till's face turn black with anger. He whirled around, lifted his flask, and drew on it long and hard till it was empty. Then he said, "You can keep your sermons for yourself!" He flung the bottle toward the board fence behind which I was hiding at the time. It hit with a crash, broke into a thousand pieces of fine glass, and scared me half to smithereens.

But I never forgot and never would.

Everybody around Sugar Creek knew what a difference Dan Browne's becoming a Christian had made in his family. People never got over talking about it. Mr. Browne never did either, and sometimes he'd get an invitation to speak in a church or a school assembly or even in the county jail.

His talk would nearly always be called "Trailing Trash."

"Whenever a dog leaves a trail for something the hunter doesn't want, it's called trailing trash," he would tell them. "I've trailed a lot of trash in my day—staying away from church without a good reason I could give to God, using profanity, being unfair to my wife or children, buying booze instead of shoes . . ."

He certainly was well trained now, all right, just as he'd trained his hounds. Old Jay and Bawler were so good and so well trained that sometimes Dan would get a call from another state to bring his dogs and track down something or other that was killing sheep or cattle or too many deer.

Once a wealthy rancher from out West came to Sugar Creek in his private plane. He flew Circus's dad to his ranch to help him catch a mountain lion that was raiding his corral and stealing one lamb after another.

The morning Mr. Browne left for Parke County, he stopped his pickup at our house to ask Mom to be sure to phone his wife several times every day. "We're getting a new baby at our house next month," I heard him say.

I was standing near the mailbox admiring his long-nosed, long-eared, sad-faced hounds, Jay and Bawler, leashed in the back of the pickup. Ichabod was in the front seat with Circus, who was holding onto his collar, trying to calm him down. "You going, too?" I asked Circus.

"Just this far," Circus said. "Ichy would get his eyes scratched out and his ears slit to ribbons if he ever got into a fight with Old Stubtail. He's got to get experience catching coons first—and they're bad enough."

Pretty soon Circus was out of the pickup, and Ichabod was putting up a noisy fuss to get in the back with his mother and old Jay. But Circus didn't let him. "You can't go!" Circus scolded and held onto his collar. "You stay home with me and be a good boy, and we'll let you catch a baby coon. There's a nest of them down in the old elm above the papaw bushes. Understand?"

Ichabod didn't understand, and he kept on trying to get up where his mother was.

Just before Mr. Browne drove away, I heard Mom say to him, "Bill's expecting a new cousin in Memory City before long, too. I've promised to be there to help celebrate. But it'll be several weeks yet, and you'll be home before that, so I can phone your wife every day you're gone."

But it *wasn't* several weeks. It wasn't even several days. Early the very next morning, the phone rang. It wasn't an emergency ring, but it *was* an emergency. Wally, my city cousin, was going to get his new baby sister or brother that very day, and Mom was supposed to come right away to help celebrate.

In less time almost than it takes me to write it, Mom had Charlotte Ann and herself ready and in the car. Dad was also in, and they were ready to start.

Even though my baby cousin was going to be born that day in Memory City, *I* wasn't going to get to go. I had to stay home to finish the morning chores, to hoe the potatoes in the little patch that belonged to me, and to do the chores in the evening just in case for some reason Dad didn't get home in time to do them with me.

Old Jersey, our one milk cow, had to be milked twice a day. And the other stock had to be fed, including the six little pigs in the straw with their mother—although they could feed themselves.

From behind the wheel of the car, my dad gave me my final orders. "I'd rather you didn't use your new rifle for target practice while I'm away."

"Yes sir," I said and felt sad and glad at the same time—glad all over that I had a rifle of my own and sad that Dad didn't think I was big enough to know how to use it all by myself.

"Another thing," Dad said above the whirring of the engine, "in case of rain, close all the windows in the house. And as soon as the chickens are all in tonight, be sure to shut the henhouse door."

Mom had a few instructions, too. "Your dinner is on the stove. Just warm it up. And while I'm gone, you and your father wash the dishes at least once a day."

They were off in a whirl of dust, leaving me to myself for what would probably be a whole day. It might even be after dark before Dad could get back.

I watched the car until it disappeared, and I watched the cloud of dust it had raised until the wind had blown it into nothing in the direction of Bumblebee Hill. Then I went into the house to the phone by the east window and turned the crank, two shorts and a long.

When Poetry's mother answered, I asked for Poetry himself.

She called him in a loud, motherlike voice. While I was waiting for him to come from wherever he was, his mother said to me, "I suppose you want my son to come over and keep you company while you're all alone today?"

"How'd you know?" I asked.

And she answered, "A little bird told me."

I knew she probably meant she'd accidentally had her phone receiver off the hook when Mom was talking to Wally's father long distance.

When Poetry answered, he was very mysterious in his tone of voice. "Listen," he hissed, "I've got a secret. You'd never guess what."

"What?" I asked.

And he answered in his still-mysterious voice, "I'll tell you this afternoon while down at the mouth of the branch, fishing."

"I've got to hoe potatoes," I objected. "I'm not sure I'll let me go fishing."

"Your folks are gone to Memory City, aren't they?"

"Yes, but—"

"All right then. I'll meet you with my secret at two o'clock. At the mouth of the branch."

"Why don't you come over right now?" I asked. "You could help me hoe the potatoes, and we could get done faster and catch more fish sooner."

His answer didn't have any mystery in its tone of voice. It was "I have a father."

We set the time for two o'clock then, and I started off on the run to finish the morning chores and to get the potato patch cleaned of every weed there was.

Really, it felt good to work, something I was beginning to like to do, for some reason.

Maybe it was because Mom and Dad had been bragging on me a little for being so thoughtful around the house and farm. Or else it was because I'd proved for the past six weeks that I *could* be thoughtful, that I *could* get up in the morning without being called three times, that I *could* actually take my Saturday night bath without being told to four times—such things as that. To reward me, Dad had bought me a beautiful new .22 Savage rifle.

To earn it, he told me, I'd have to prove I could take responsibility. I would have to show him I could act even older than my age. Also I'd had to learn by heart, word for word, "The Ten Commandments of Hunting Safety" and to pass a written examination on it. A *written* examination, mind you, just like a boy takes in school!

But I'd passed with an almost perfect grade, and it had felt so good to actually *be* good that I was sort of keeping on, like a wound-up clock.

I decided to surprise my parents by cleaning up the yard before starting on the potatoes.

Every time I stopped to rest and went into the house for cookies or something, I looked up longingly at my .22. I took it down several times and wished Dad hadn't thought to tell me not to do any target practice while he was away.

Once, just to be sure I had not broken one of the most important rules of hunting safety, I opened the breach to see if I had left it unloaded. I was glad I had, because one of the rules is *never* to leave a loaded gun unattended. I patted its shining walnut stock, stroked its blue steel barrel, and said to it, calling it by the name I'd given it the day Dad bought it for me, "Betty Lizzie, one of these days you're going to come in handy. You'll maybe save my life in an emergency."

When the chores and the hoeing were done, I picked up my bait can, which would have been perfect for setting on a fence post and using for a target, took my long cane fishing pole, and went out the front gate, passing "Theodore Collins" on our mailbox. My bare feet went *plop-plop-ploppety-plop-plop* in the dust of the gravel road on the way to meet my best friend, who said he was bringing a mystery with him.

Since there wasn't any wildcat in the territory for a boy to be scared of, the gang would have to think up something else interesting to talk about and to be a little worried about.

Life's a lot more interesting if there is a mystery around or something exciting or a bit dangerous. For that reason, I hated to think of Old Stubtail's being so far away. A boy ought to have a chance to find out how good a shot he is and whether a bullet from a .22 could really kill a wildcat.

"Ho hum," I yawned as I went lazily along, wondering if maybe I'd catch a fish or two before Poetry came.

I must have eaten too much of the boiled dinner Mom had left for me. I had warmed it up and eaten several large helpings. I certainly felt sleepy. In a few minutes I'd be at the mouth of the branch, where there was a nice grassy place to stretch out and take a nap while the wriggling, twisting angleworms tempted the fish to bite away down in the water on the end of my hook.

It certainly was quiet around Sugar Creek —too quiet for a boy.

Too, *too* quiet. Almost as quiet as it is sometimes just before there is a big thunderstorm. As quiet as a cat sneaking up on a mouse.

How was I to know, as I baited my hook and tossed my line out into the lazy water, that even though nobody around Sugar Creek had reported any killings by Old Stubtail and even though some farmers in Parke County a hundred miles away had lost a few sheep and other livestock—how was I to know that great big twenty-eight toothed, savage-tempered wildcat was still hanging around our territory? How was I to know that sleepy afternoon was to be the beginning of more excitement than the gang had had in a long time?

3

As you maybe know, the mouth of the branch is·not far from the sycamore tree and the cave where we'd had so many interesting experiences. I was glad that Poetry wasn't already there with his mystery, because sometimes his mysteries turned out to be just his imagination stretched too far.

Besides, I wasn't in the mood to get really excited about anything. It was too lazy a day for even a hungry fish to bite, I thought. I did put on several of the juiciest worms I had in my bait can, and pretty soon I was stretched out in the sun watching my bottle-cork bobber lying lazily on the foam-specked water.

I waited and waited for a bite, waiting also for Poetry. It wasn't two o'clock yet by nearly fifteen minutes. My bobber was as lifeless as I felt, and the slow-moving foam clusters kept on drifting past it, while a half-dozen devil's darning needle dragonflies skimmed all over the water like baby-sized, four-winged airplanes looking for a landing field. They kept coming and going, almost making me dizzy.

I was too drowsy to care whether I got a bite, and I hoped my barrel-shaped best friend would stay away until I'd had a nice little snooze.

My nodding head woke me up just enough

to remind me I'd better set my pole good and tight in case I actually *did* go to sleep. If some lazy fish down there in the water somewhere should wake up and yawn, swallow the juicy wriggling cluster of angleworms with my sharp-barbed hook in them, feel the barb, and suddenly start running wildly in every direction out into deeper water—if *that* should happen while I was sleeping, the big savage fish might pull my pole in after it.

I was on my back now, my head resting on a stone pillow, which I had made more comfortable by covering it with my jacket. I pulled my straw hat over my eyes to shade them from the sun and its light, yawned several noisy yawns, sighed several sighs, and let my lazy thoughts drift away into nothing.

It seemed I was seeing Wynken, Blynken, and Nod sailing about the sky in a wooden shoe in the poem every boy knows, which was written by Eugene Field and is in one of the books in our school library. Then I was *in* the wooden shoe with Wynken, Blynken, and Nod, sailing higher and higher, past the moon and stars. I was fishing in a sea of dew.

Was I actually asleep? I wondered.

Just then I became aware of the stone pillow under my head. And one of the Bible stories I'd heard Dad read—and which you already know about—started roaming about in my mind. If I was dreaming, I thought, then I certainly wasn't red-haired Bill Collins, who didn't have any brother to fight with but had only a red-haired city cousin who had a city-bred, ill-mannered mongrel of a dog that wasn't afraid of anything but would rush in where an ordinary dog would be scared to even bark.

In my dream, if it was a dream, now it seemed I was Jacob, who had had a quarrel with his brother, Esau, and had run away to keep from getting killed. It seemed to be night, and I was in a very rocky place where there were wildcats hiding in caves and going up and down a gold stairway like a department store escalator.

Then in my dream I heard a voice from the top of the ladder calling down to me, saying, "The land on which you lie, I will give it to you . . ."

It was a very strong, very kind, very deep-echoing voice, different from any I had ever heard. It seemed it was the voice of God, who had made all the wonderful things in nature—the creek and the birds, the rocks and rills, the woods and templed hills, all the boys there are in the world—and even the girls.

I had *felt* the voice many a time in my heart but had never before *heard* it. It sounded like organ music in the Sugar Creek church and like water in the riffles and like the friendly thunder after a storm. It made me think of a hand slowly stroking the soft fur of a kitten . . .

And then is when I woke up.

I had heard a strange sound close by, I thought, a sound that scared me all to smithereens.

A fast wind was ruffling the surface of the

creek. My brown bottle-cork bobber was zigzagging around as if I was getting a whopper of a bite, and in the direction of the swamp there was the excited rumble of actual thunder. The sun was smothered under a cover of worried, dark brown clouds, and there was the smell of rain in the air. I must have slept quite a while, I thought.

That was when I heard another sound and saw what had made it. Sitting on the trunk of the big elm overhanging the water was a great furry animal. It looked like a giant-sized tiger cat, ten times as big as Mixy, the Collins family's house cat. But this cat didn't have any nice, long, bushy tail. It had a stub about eight inches long.

I guess I'd never come so wide awake so fast in my life. The fierce-looking animal was crouching in my direction, snarling now. He held one wide front foot on the bloody carcass of what was left of a half-eaten rabbit.

I saw the angry gray-green eyes glaring at me as if I had interrupted his dinner. I heard him spit and hiss the way Mixy spits and hisses when she's angry or has been interrupted in her eating.

In that fleeting flash of a few seconds, I saw the brown stripes on his forehead, the long gray-white whiskers, the whitish chin and throat. The huge claw-filled paw holding down the remains of the bunny looked as though it was powerful enough to rip a dog's ears to shreds with one fierce, fast thrust.

I was sitting up, which means I must have awakened with such a start that I was halfway up before realizing it—as a boy sometimes does even when he is home and safe in a nice warm bed.

Now, I managed to think, would be a good time to see how fast I could run toward Theodore Collins's house and a good time to try out a .22 Savage on a savage wild animal. It certainly wouldn't be disobeying Dad to kill Old Stubtail, because that wouldn't be target practice at all.

I was on my feet in a flash, ready to start a speedy sprint toward the branch bridge and across it on the way to get Betty Lizzie.

Then's when I caught a glimpse of my fishing line cutting a wide circle in the water. The cane pole was bouncing as though I had a fish as big as a wildcat on it.

I dove for the pole, grabbed it, felt the wild-running fish on the other end of the line, forgot about being scared of the wildcat, and in a few fast, not-very-skillful movements had landed a whopper of a largemouth bass. I remembered while I was doing it that fish bite better when it's raining or going to rain.

And right then I heard another roll of thunder—not in the distance but a lot closer. I hurried to get the bass off the hook and onto the stringer I'd brought. I wasn't able to feel proud of myself for catching him on account of the wildcat's being not more than twenty-five feet from me on the overhanging elm trunk.

Anybody knows a boy can't feel proud and scared half to death at the same time.

I knew, of course, that wildcats eat mice and rabbits and small birds but wouldn't attack a human being unless they were cornered or thought they were. I certainly wasn't going to get close enough to the base of the overhanging tree to make Old Stubtail think I was after him—that he was cornered—and to run the risk of having him spring at me.

But why let him scare me out of what few wits I had? I didn't have to let him keep me from catching another big fish or setting my pole again. I quick baited the hook with a half dozen of the biggest, juiciest, liveliest worms in the target practice can.

Then, I tied the free end of my stringer onto a willow by the shore and eased the whopper of a bass I'd already caught into the water at the edge, so he'd stay alive. In a jiffy now, my pole would be set, and I'd be flying home for Betty Lizzie. I might even get the savage-looking wildcat killed before Poetry came.

And that's when I heard a boy's squawky, ducklike voice calling from the direction of the branch bridge. Seconds later, the boy behind the voice broke through the bushes. It was Poetry, running like a barrel with legs on it, carrying a large, rectangular brown envelope.

That, also, is when the wind blew hard and it began to rain.

"Come on!" he yelled to me. "Let's get to the cave, or we'll be drowned! There's a terrible storm coming up!" He shoved the brown envelope inside his shirt to keep it from getting wet.

"Look!" I cried to him and pointed toward the overhanging tree. "There's a wildcat up there! Old Stubtail's back again! He's up there eating a rabbit!"

"Where?" He looked toward where I was pointing.

"Right up there . . . right . . . right . . ."

But there wasn't any wildcat with fierce face and savage claws glaring down at us. And there wasn't any half-eaten bloody carcass of a rabbit.

What on earth, I thought.

Poetry irked me into getting almost fighting mad at him when he said sarcastically, "Oh yeah! A wildcat or a wild idea?"

Then it did begin to rain. There was a roaring in the trees overhead and all around. A blinding lightning flash and an explosion of thunder ten times louder than a rifle shot came at the same time. My mind screamed for me to get out of there in a hurry—away from any tall trees, which are dangerous to be under when there's an electrical storm.

Gritting my teeth at being made fun of by my best friend and having my word doubted, I cried to him, "There *was* a wildcat up there eating a rabbit! He was spitting and hissing, and his right front paw had curving claws that could scratch a dog's eyes out and tear his ear to shreds in one fierce, fast stroke!"

But where *was* the furry animal that had

been there only a few exciting minutes ago? I knew I'd seen him. *Knew* it!

There wasn't time now to argue, and arguing wouldn't do any good anyway. We had to get to the cave quick or get as wet as if we'd fallen in the creek.

Our four bare feet flew over the path we'd run on a thousand times in our lives—in fact, almost a thousand times that very summer, toward the sycamore tree and the cave.

The wildcat would get wet, too, I thought. And in my mind's eye I saw our old black and white cat at home. Whenever she was outdoors and it started to rain, she would come to cat life fast and run like a scared rabbit to the house or toolshed or would streak like a four-legged arrow across the barnyard to the hole under the barn.

"Maybe wildcats are like pussycats," I thought out loud. "Maybe Old Stubtail hurried down the tree to get in out of the rain."

"Yeah." Poetry puffed his reply as he lumbered along behind me. "Maybe he's outrun us and is already in the cave!"

"Cave!" my mind and my voice screamed at the same time.

It was an exciting idea—and a scary one. Maybe Old Stubtail *had* gone to the cave to get in out of the rain. Maybe he had made it his home already and had his den there. Maybe after he lost the dogs up in the hills, he'd circle back through the swamp and hide in his secret place in our cave!

It took two fast-running boys only a half-dozen wet minutes to get to the sycamore tree with its white and purple and gray bark—which I didn't even bother to notice—and inside the black, open mouth of the cave. There we stopped, panting for breath, and looked back out at the rain that was coming down in sheets. We heard the roaring wind and saw the trees whipping hard.

There were a lot of things on my mind right then: the strange and very wonderful dream of the golden escalator leading up to the skies; the voice I'd heard in the dream; the whopper of a bass I'd caught and which, right that minute, was on the end of the stringer in the creek; the angry eyes of the wildcat; Poetry's doubting my words, calling them a wild idea; the storm that had driven us here; and especially, the wildcat's being gone when I'd pointed out to Poetry where he'd been.

It certainly was storming hard. There was wind, jagged lightning, deafening thunder, and blinding sheets of rain.

I tried telling Poetry over again about what I'd seen, but he still didn't believe me. "Old Stubtail's down in Parke County. Don't you remember? Circus's father and old Jay and Bawler left yesterday to go down and catch him!"

"But I saw him when I woke up!" I protested. I told Poetry about going to sleep and all of a sudden waking up with the wind blowing and low clouds scudding across the sky. I told him about the whopper of a bass I'd caught—and the wildcat eating the rabbit.

But his mind was like an up umbrella in the rain. My words fell on him and rolled off.

"All right," I said, "call me a liar."

"You're not a liar," he defended me. "You just have an elastic imagination. You *thought* you saw it. You just said yourself you'd been asleep and the wind woke you up!"

I *had* just said that to him, but I certainly didn't expect him to take my words, make a whip out of them, and give me a switching.

There wasn't much of anything we could do in the cave while we waited for the storm to stop, and it was pretty dark in there because there wasn't any sunshine outside. The wind kept whipping the trees outside the cave, and the thunder and lightning were acting as though they were mad at each other and at the whole world.

I was still thinking about Old Stubtail. I *knew* I'd seen and heard him. I wondered what had become of him. In my mind now was an idea that had come to me a little while before. Old Stubtail might *really* have run to the cave to get in out of the rain! He might be here right now, not more than a few feet from us!

All of a sudden I heard something behind me that started my hair to crawling on the back of my neck.

"Hear that!" I whispered huskily. "That's him! That's Old Stubtail! He's back in the cave somewhere behind us."

4

I was more scared now than I had been back at the base of the leaning elm on whose trunk I'd seen the wildcat.

It's not nearly as frightening to *see* a dangerous wild animal when you're quite a distance from it as it is to be in a dark cave and *hear* one behind you somewhere—and you can't see it.

The roar of the storm didn't make it any easier for us to hear what we were trying to hear.

Scratch . . . scratch . . . I'd heard.

We knew that the other end of the cave came out away up in the hills in the basement of Old Man Paddler's cabin, but what we were hearing was close by. Very close. Not more than six feet from us, it seemed.

I'd never seen Poetry so calm at a time like that. "We'll find out in one minute if there's anything back in there anywhere," he said.

And then I saw that he had out his waterproof matchbox, the one he nearly always carried with him. He struck a match and lit one of the candles we kept on a shelf in a holder. We'd lit candles there many a time when we'd had gang meetings.

"Now," he said, "we'll—"

Then we *did* hear something for sure.

"It's behind the wall here somewhere," I said. "It's the wildcat, I tell you! He's got his den here in the cave! That's why he wasn't on the tree when I tried to show you he was! He knew the storm was coming and made a bee-line for here!"

Just saying it made it seem actually the truth, and I was cringing aplenty.

Poetry's face in the light of the candle showed that he was a little afraid himself, but he wasn't the kind of boy to admit it. "Let's have a look," he said, and he held the candle close to the wall where we'd heard the sound. Then he let out a heavy, disgruntled sigh and said, "Well, that's that. There's a leak in the cave roof. That's all. See the water dripping?"

I'd already seen, and my ears were already hearing. *Drip . . . drip . . . drip* instead of *scratch . . . scratch . . . scratch . . .*

While we were still waiting for the storm to subside, we used the light of the candle to help us see to put together Poetry's space patrol periscope, which was his mystery and what was in the brown envelope.

First, we took it out, cleaned the two mirrors, one at either end, as the directions for assembling it said, and step by step we put it together. It'd be fun to use, making us able to see around corners without being seen, look over the tops of people's heads to watch a parade, or over the stone fence at the cemetery while we ourselves would be on the other side. There'd be a lot of uses for it.

I was still irked at my best friend, though, for not believing me about the whopper of a cat I'd seen. Of course, I'd seen him! I hadn't been just dreaming, I was sure. I'd also caught a whopper of a bass, and I knew I wasn't dreaming when I'd done that. I had proof of it on the stringer tied to the willow down by the mouth of the branch.

I began to feel a little better toward Poetry, though, as we worked together on the periscope. *After all, he's my best friend,* I thought. We'd had more fun and trouble together than any two of the rest of the gang.

"As soon as this storm is over," he announced, "we'll go back to where you saw your little kitty and look for clues. If we find blood on the tree trunk where he was chewing on the rabbit, we'll know you weren't asleep."

And then I was mad again. I gritted my teeth and said, "OK, chum, have it your way. We'll find the blood. It'll be there, all right."

As soon as we were sure the storm was over, we went out in the rainwashed air and splashed our way down the muddy path to the mouth of the branch where I'd seen the "kitty" and where my whopper of a bass was on the stringer, tied to the willow not far from the base of the leaning elm.

Poetry worked his way carefully along the slanting trunk of the tree so as not to fall off the slippery wet bark, and I stood grinning, expecting him any minute to find a little blood or some bits of rabbit fur to prove I was right.

"Nothing here," he called back. "Not even a scratch on the bark. Not a single claw mark."

I called up to him, "Then the rain washed the blood off, and if there was any rabbit fur, it washed off into the creek and floated downstream!"

At least he'd have to believe me about the whopper of a bass I'd caught. I'd been bragging about that to him, too.

"OK," I said. "Come on down, and I'll let you carry my bass home."

I caught hold of the end of the stringer, not untying it first because I wanted to hold up the whopper for Poetry to see without running the risk of its getting away.

Then I felt a sinking sensation in the pit of my stomach. There wasn't any big largemouth bass on the end of the stringer! There wasn't *anything*. The stringer was empty.

"What on earth!" I exclaimed

"I will be in a minute!" Poetry called down from the place on the tree trunk where the wildcat had been and now wasn't.

We stood for a few seconds looking at my empty stringer.

I could feel what Poetry was thinking before he let out a grunt and said, "The wildcat that wasn't there ate a whopper of a bass that wasn't there that had been caught by a red-haired, freckled-faced boy that wasn't *all* there!" —meaning he thought I wasn't quite bright.

Before I could even start to prove to him that I was, he grunted again, caught the stringer by its empty end, studied it a minute, and said in his ducklike voice, "Or maybe the *bunny* that hadn't been there ate the fish that wasn't there that was caught by the boy that wasn't—"

That was as far as he got. I chopped his sentence in two by exploding at him. "If the barrel-shaped boy had been there, there wouldn't have been room enough for anything else!"

It wasn't a very kind thing to say. Extra-heavy people shouldn't be made fun of unless they do it themselves. My parents had taught me that. They were always careful not to hurt anybody's feelings.

I untied the stringer from the willow, hardly able to see it on account of the crazy tears that were in my eyes. Now I was *really* angry at my best friend—not so much because he was making fun of me but because I couldn't prove to him there *had* been a wildcat eating a bunny, which there actually *had* been, and because there wasn't even any whopper of a large-mouth bass on the stringer, which I myself had caught and put there.

Well, it was time for me to go home and start the evening chores, and it was also time for Poetry to go home. I knew it was for sure when I heard, from away up near their house, his mother's voice calling in a high-pitched tremolo that sounded like Ichabod's long wail. The way her call echoed through the woods sent chills up and down my spine. For a second it seemed I was running with the gang, following the hounds on a hot wildcat trail.

Always mischievous-minded, Poetry swung his periscope up to his eyes and looked into the small round hole at the bottom, saying at the same time, "Maybe I can see your little kitty by looking in here."

Of course, he couldn't.

His mother called again, and this time her tremolo sounded as if *she* was on a hot trail.

Poetry let out a yell back and started on a fast run along the wet path toward the branch bridge and on toward home.

I myself went on toward the Theodore Collins house, carrying the sad-looking empty stringer and my long cane fishing pole—and with an empty feeling in my heart.

It was a sad, wet walk. The rain had poured down so hard that little rivulets were running in the gravel road. There was muddy water everywhere. There were green leaves all over, too, blown from the trees, and quite a few fallen branches. The storm must have been even worse than it had seemed while we were in the cave.

Inside the house, I took a quick half-sad, half-glad look up at Betty Lizzie on her rack above the closed east door. I was certainly glad I had left that door closed, and also the window by the phone, because the wind had come from the east and we would have had water all over the floor. It wasn't any credit to me, though, since the door and that east window had already been closed when I'd gone fishing.

I took a quick look-run-see all over the house upstairs and down to be sure there wasn't any water on the floor anywhere or on the beds, and I felt a little better that there wasn't any.

While I was still upstairs, our phone rang one long and one short. It was our ring.

That'll be Poetry, I thought. *He wants to make up. He's sorry he teased me.*

But instead, it was long distance. Dad was calling from Memory City. The celebration at Wally's house hadn't started yet. There also had been a bad electrical storm there, and several bridges were out. He wanted to know if I was all right.

I was glad to tell Dad I was and that the rain hadn't rained into the house anywhere.

Mom got on the phone then. There'd been a little change in their plans. She told me I could either stay all night at Poetry's or he could come and stay with me, because Dad was going to wait till morning to start home.

My heart was pounding because I wasn't used to long-distance phone calls. But a little later when I hung up, I felt good inside—as if I'd done something important.

I picked up the receiver again, took hold of the crank handle of the phone with my other hand, and got ready to ring two shorts and a long to ask Poetry to come and stay all night at my house.

I got the two shorts rung before I remembered I was still mad at him, and I quick hung up. I didn't need any barrel-shaped baby-sitter to look after me. Any boy who was old enough to own a rifle and could catch a whopper of a bass and—my thoughts stopped bragging on me when I remembered the bass had been off the stringer instead of *on* it.

Had I actually been dreaming? I wondered for the first time.

Right now, as I stood again in the kitchen looking up at Betty Lizzie, it seemed there had not only been a wildcat on the leaning tree eating a rabbit and a big bass running wild on the other end of my line, but there had also been a wooden shoe as big as a boat. I'd been in it, sailing in a sea of dew past the moon, and there had been an escalator with angels and wildcats riding up and down on it.

Good sense, if I really had any, told me the wooden-shoe boat and the angels on the escalator had been only a dream, but the wildcat and the bunny and the whopper of a large-mouth bass had been real.

But I *did* have to get the chores done, so I put myself to work doing them.

When I went to bed in my upstairs south room, I lay there for a few minutes listening to the whispering of the ivy leaves at the window and the different night sounds in the woods, I was feeling quite a bit better in my mind. There was an ache at my heart, though, that my best friend hadn't believed me and also that he hadn't called up to tell me he was sorry and that he *did* believe me.

Something was pulling at me to get out of bed, go down to the phone, and ring two shorts and a long for Poetry to come over and stay with me. It was still early enough, I thought, and there was moonlight enough for him to bike his way over.

But I was stubborn, so I lay there on my soft white pillow and felt disgusted and worried a little. I wondered if any of the usual night sounds outside in the woods were unusual and if any of them were made by Old Stubtail, who wasn't there.

In the middle of the night I was awakened by something. I didn't know what. But I was so startled by whatever it was that I was sitting up in bed before I knew it, my heart pounding. Out in our chicken house there was such a squawking and cackling that I sprang from my bed to see what was the matter.

5

I had no sooner sprung from my bed to see what was the matter out in our chicken house than I thought I heard a different kind of noise near Red Addie's apartment. I strained my eyes into the shadowy moonlight. The moon was in its last quarter so was only a silvery sliver hanging in the sky over the south pasture. The shadow of the barn covered all of Addie's pig house and lot and part of the chicken yard, so I couldn't really see what was the matter.

My mind's eye was seeing right through the chicken house wall, though, and imagining a tufted-eared, leering-eyed, stub-tailed wildcat making short work of one of Mom's best laying hens. He might even be eating Old Bentcomb herself, my favorite white leghorn, who always made her nest under a log up in our haymow. She would make a tasty midnight snack for a hungry forty-five-pound monster of a cat, I thought.

Since Dad was away in Memory City and wouldn't be home till tomorrow sometime, it'd be up to me, Bill Collins, to save our flock of hens. Also, it would give me a chance to use Betty Lizzie for something besides target practice.

The excitement in the henhouse was getting noisier every second, which meant the whole flock was scared half to death about something.

I shoved myself into my overalls and, without bothering to put on a shirt over my pajama top, scurried down the stairs and into the kitchen.

I would light my way with Dad's powerful flashlight. It'd be silly to run any real risk, I thought. Old Stubtail, seeing me, might decide a red-haired boy would be just right for dessert. In a jiffy I had Betty Lizzie down and loaded. I eased my way out the back screen door and onto the board walk.

And then I heard a sound that made me stop stock-still and cringe. It was the harsh scream of a hen, sounding as if she was being murdered.

That settled that. I, Bill Collins, the head of our empty house, was going into action. I held Betty Lizzie ready to shoot if I had to. Any minute now, some wild animal might come charging out of the henhouse in my direction. But even in the middle of all that excitement, I remembered rules seven and eight of the Ten Commandments for Hunting Safety: "Be sure of your target before you fire; never point a gun at anything you don't intend to shoot. Make sure of your partner's location before firing at anything. Don't hunt with more than one companion."

I was as far as the grape arbor when the harsh-screaming hen's voice stopped as though it had been choked off, which probably meant one of our hens was dead. But the excited cackling of the other chickens was still going on.

I shot a beam from the flashlight straight toward the open henhouse door. Open! And I had been ordered by Theodore Collins to close it!

I swung the flashlight back toward Addie the pig's apartment and thought I saw—I couldn't tell for sure—a long, gray-brown shadow stalking the pen. Then for sure I saw a pair of fiery eyes, like two small flashlights, shining back on me.

Just to be sure it wasn't two flashlights, I turned mine off and those two went out. That meant I actually *had* seen the two eyes of some kind of animal reflected in my flashlight's light.

The gray-brown shadowy thing went slinking along the garden fence toward the pignut trees and disappeared in the direction of Poetry's dad's woods.

I had seen Old Stubtail again! I was positively, absolutely sure of it! I, myself, Bill Collins, who was absolutely wide awake and not dreaming, had seen him with my own wide-awake eyes!

I hadn't realized it, but I had Betty Lizzie pointed toward Addie's home. I'd swung the rifle in an arc, following the flight of the shadow. My arms were tired of holding it in a pointing position. I was trembling all over.

But I was glad I hadn't pulled the trigger, for when I sent a beam of light in the direction of the pignut trees, it came to focus on old Jersey, our milk cow, lying on her side there, chewing her cud. We might have had a dead milk cow instead of a stub-tailed wildcat.

Well, there was still a lot of excitement in the henhouse, so I decided to go over and shut the door, hoping the chickens would calm down a little and I could go back to bed and try to go to sleep.

First, I shone my light through the open door and onto the four-foot-high roosts. "Listen, girls," I said in a half-comforting, half-scolding voice, "there's nothing more to worry about. Go on back to sleep! Old Stubtail's gone, and I'm going to shut your door and latch it."

But the whole flock seemed still to be nervous. Maybe my light was bothering them, I thought. I turned it off and spoke again. "Calm down! There's nothing to be afraid of. Here, I'll prove it to you."

I swung the light in a circle all around the ceiling and the roosts and then onto the dirt floor under the old walnut table on which Mom had placed a few nests in little square boxes.

And that was when I saw what was causing all the excitement. There, in a corner under the table, was a long, gray animal the size of a house cat. It had a long, gray-brown, naked tail. Its head was long too, and slender, its eyes beady, its large ears without fur on them, and it was gnawing away on a bloody-necked white leghorn pullet.

"Possum!" I exclaimed. It wasn't a very big one and wasn't anything to be scared of—not for a boy with a gun. The gang had caught quite a few of them when we'd been hunting with Circus's dad's hounds. The dogs hardly ever trailed one but *sometimes* did and got scolded for it if they had already been on a coon trail and had gotten off. I had even picked up a half-dozen possums by their long, prehensile tails.

I shone Dad's flashlight full into Opi's grinning face—Opi was the name the gang had for any possum we happened to see. True to a possum's nature at a time like that, he curled himself up into a ball, opened his mouth, showed a long row of pretty, white teeth, and lay on his side, absolutely still.

I quickly stooped, lifted him by his tail, and carried him outside.

He didn't seem to like that. He came to life for a minute, struggled to get his head up to bite my hand, then gave up and went back to his pretended sleep.

It was only a possum, and it wasn't possum hunting season anyway, so I carried him to the orchard fence, dropped him over on the other side, and ordered him, "You stay out of our chicken house, do you hear!"

And that was that.

I went back, got what was left of Opi's midnight lunch, and carried it to the orchard fence, too. I tossed it over, where it fell under one of Dad's Early Elberta peach trees. Tomorrow I would bury it somewhere so that the blue-bottle flies wouldn't come and lay their eggs all over it.

Even though I knew that the screwworms that would hatch from the bluebottle eggs were what Dad called "scavengers" and if given enough time would eat up the whole chicken carcass, he larvae would grow into more bluebottle flies —and there were already too many of those.

Besides, I remembered that sometimes blue-bottle flies laid their eggs in a cut or open sore of farm animals, and then the larvae ate the living tissues as well as the dead and caused a lot of deaths in cattle country, especially in the southern part of the United States.

So it's a good thing to kill or trap every bluebottle fly you can. Don't even let even a housefly live if you can help it.

Back to the chicken house door I went again and shut it tight and bolted it.

Still worried about what I'd seen—or *thought* I'd seen—at Addie's gate, I shot my light out there again. And what to my wondering eyes should appear but two fiery eyes again! It was something with black and white fur this time, though! It was Mixy nosing around the gate and arching her lazy back against the post.

What a disappointment!

First, I had thought there was a wildcat in the chicken house, and it had turned out to be a possum eating a leghorn pullet. And now the wildcat I thought I'd seen at Addie's pig house had turned out to be a tame house cat that was wild only when in a hissing, spitting, scratching fight with a dog.

A few minutes before, when I had seen the fiery eyes of that gray something-or-other stealing along the garden fence toward the pignut trees, I'd felt almost happy in spite of being scared. I was sure there was a wildcat in the neighborhood, that Old Stubtail had come back from Parke County. In the afternoon, when I was down at the mouth of the branch, I *hadn't* been dreaming when I saw a rabbit being eaten by a tufted-eared, angry-eyed wild animal of the cat family.

I called Mixy, and she came running toward me in a half-awkward lope the way cats do. I looked down at her blinking eyes and growled at her grumpily, "It's your fault for scaring me! I'm disgusted!"

She meowed a lazy meow up at me, arched her back, pushed against my pant leg, and walked past. Then she started off on a cat trot toward the iron pitcher pump and the place where she knew her milk pan was, inviting me to come and feed her a midnight lunch.

I stood awhile, thinking while feeling the cool night breeze on my pajama-clad arms. I sighed heavily, took a squint at the moon, felt sleepy, and thought for a second about the poem "Wynken, Blynken, and Nod." I yawned my way through one of the stanzas I had memorized, which was:

"'Where are you going, and what do you
    wish?'
The old moon asked the three.
'We have come to fish for the herring fish
That live in this beautiful sea.'"

There was another line that started out
"The old moon laughed and sang a song . . ." I
couldn't remember the rest of it. But as I kept
on looking at the little sliver of a moon, it
seemed it was shaped like a silver mouth that
was laughing at me for being such a scared
goose.

Disappointed and sleepy, I carried Betty
Lizzie into the house, unloaded her, went back
upstairs, undressed, and was soon in bed with
Wynken, Blynken, and Nod.

I tried to remember the whole poem, saying it over in my mind. But I didn't get very far
—only about as far as the place where it says,

"Wynken and Blynken are two little eyes
    [fiery eyes, I thought]
    And Nod is a little head."

The next thing I knew it was morning, and
the telephone downstairs was ringing one long
and one short, the number everybody on the
party line knew was ours.

6

For a second I thought the ringing phone was Dad's alarm clock and that I'd have a while to sleep before he'd start calling me to come down to help him with the chores.

I was back with Wynken, Blynken, and Nod in a sea of dew, when the phone rang again. In a flash I realized nobody was home except me, and it'd be up to me to go down and answer it—which I did.

It wasn't anything very important, except that I was supposed to go over to Poetry's house for the noon meal that day. Dad was invited, too.

"He's not home yet," I said to Poetry's mother.

"Not home yet!" she exclaimed. "I thought he was coming back last night!"

"He phoned me he'd not be here till today sometime," I answered her.

Then her voice sounded really astonished. "You mean you stayed all night alone there— all by yourself?"

Because I always liked to have a girl or a woman feel worried about me or think I was brave, I said, "Well, not exactly alone. I had our old cat, six little pigs, a possum, and a wildcat. But don't worry. I'm all right."

"Oh, you!" she said, then added, "I'll send Poetry over right away to help with the chores."

"No, *don't!*" I said. "I can get along very nicely without—" I wanted to say, "I can get along very nicely without a barrel-shaped boy who thinks I'm an idiot and won't believe what I say." But I remembered Dad's and Mom's ideal never to hurt people's feelings if you could help it, so I added into the phone, "Thank you very much for the invitation. I'll tell Dad as soon as he gets here."

I did feel a little better toward Mrs. Thompson's barrel-shaped son, though. So a little later, when he actually did come over to help me with the chores, we started acting as if we liked each other again.

I told him all about Opi and the other excitement I'd had. Then I began to feel him doubting me again.

Since he was so mischievous most of the time anyway, I couldn't tell whether he was joking or not when he said, "Yesterday it was a wildcat eating a rabbit. Last night it was a possum eating a chicken under the table in the henhouse. How come he didn't put his food *on* the table instead of *under* it? Show me what's left of the carcass, and I'll believe you."

"OK, smarty," I said. "Right this way." I led him to the orchard fence, looked over, and told him, "Right over there under the Early Elberta peach tree. I threw the carcass right over . . . right over . . . right . . ."

I stopped saying "right," because I was

wrong. There weren't any feathered remains of one of Mom's best laying pullets—not under the peach tree or anywhere in a wide circle all around it.

What, I thought, *on earth!*

It was too much like yesterday, when there hadn't been any wildcat or any rabbit or any whopper of a bass. I'd been dreaming about that bass, and last night I'd been dreaming about herring in a sea of dew. It just didn't make sense.

Poetry stooped and picked up a white feather—a wing feather from one of Mom's hens, I supposed. He tucked it under the band of his straw hat and squawked a stanza of a song every boy knows:

> "Yankee Doodle went to town,
> Riding on a pony,
> Stuck a feather in his hat
> And called it macaroni."

Then he asked sarcastically, "How come he didn't call it baloney?"

Then Poetry got a serious expression on his face. Maybe it was because he saw the angry tears in my eyes or maybe because he was my best friend—anyway, he *had* been. He laid an arm across my shoulder and said, "If you say there was a possum, there was a possum. No reason why he couldn't have eaten the rest of the pullet or dragged it away somewhere."

I gulped, swung around, scooped up Mixy,

who was meowing at my feet, and cuddled her a little. Then I started for the toolshed to get a spade. It'd be a wonderful morning to go fishing after yesterday's rain. It might be a good idea to get started before Dad came home.

The garden was too wet to hoe potatoes anyway. It's not good for potatoes to be hoed when the ground is soaking wet.

We left a note on the kitchen table for my dad, telling him where we were and telling him about our being invited to eat raspberry pie and roast beef at Poetry's house that noon.

That was another thing I found out: The gang's mothers had made it up among them to have Dad and me eat all our noon meals at their different houses every day while Mom was in Memory City celebrating my cousin's new baby sister or brother.

It was fun digging the worms. The best place on our farm was not far from Addie's pig house. I used the spade, and Poetry used his hands to break up the big damp clods and pick up the worms.

"Angleworms or earthworms," Poetry began in what Dad would call a philosophical tone of voice, "are very helpful to the farmer. They eat dirt, swallowing it whole like fish eat fishing worms. What they can't digest, they pile up in little piles around their burrows. In this way, they bring the deeper parts of the richer soil to the surface." It sounded like something he had memorized.

It surely felt good to have him seem his

good old mischievous self again and to feel that he liked me. I knew what he was saying was the truth about earthworms, because I had learned it myself, listening to a 4-H club speaker at a meeting different ones of our fathers had taken us to.

Addie, in her pen, seemed a lot more nervous than usual. She was squealing and complaining as if she hadn't already had her breakfast of corn and tankage and a pail of milk from the separator.

Poetry stopped squawking about earthworms eating earth the way fish eat fishing worms. Looking at Addie, he began quoting in a singsong tone the little ditty he had quoted to her one other time, changing one of the lines a little to make it sound funnier:

"Six little pigs in the straw with their mother,
 Bright tails, curly eyes, tumbling on each
   other;
 Bring them apples from the orchard trees,
 And hear those piggies say, 'Please, please,
   please.'"

He started to singsong it again. Then he stopped, stared, and yelled, "I thought there were six little pigs! She's only got *five!*"

He was joking, I thought. It was a good poem to quote, cute and just right for Addie to hear. She was so proud of her frisky little curly tailed family. There were six in the poem and six in the pen.

Poetry plopped down his bait can. It fell on its side, and the squirming worms started to worm their way out in every direction there is. He quick set the can right side up, scooped up each runaway worm, and put it back in. There was a very sober expression on his face as he asked me, "How many pigs is she supposed to have?"

"Six!" I answered. "Don't you remember? You saw them the morning after they were born, the day Chuck Hammer was here!"

His answer came in a grim voice, "She's got only five now. You sure one of 'em didn't die?"

I still thought he was only pretending to be excited, so I said, "Oh, the other one'll be back in the pig house somewhere." But his excitement was like measles. It was contagious, and I was about to catch it from him. I was seeing again what I'd seen last night—two fiery eyes too wide apart and too high from the ground to have been Mixy's.

We left our spade and the can of worms and in a minute were inside the hog lot, looking all over for a cute little curly tailed rascal of a piggie that was probably taking a nap or wallowing in the mud all by himself.

We looked inside the pig house, under the straw, all around under the weeds in the lot, and there wasn't any little red-haired pig child —not in the straw with its mother or anywhere else.

All of a sudden Poetry's eyes narrowed, and for an anxious moment we stared at each other. Then he said excitedly, pointing down at a patch of chocolate-colored grass near the gate, "That looks like dried blood!"

I had been afraid to tell him what I thought I had seen at this very place last night, but now, I decided, was the time to tell. I was sure now that those two fiery eyes had belonged to Old Stubtail himself. He had really come back from Parke County.

"I saw Old Stubtail last night," I said. "He was crouching right here. When I turned my flashlight on him, he slunk away."

Poetry whistled an exclamation that said he was getting even more excited. It also seemed to say that this time he really believed me.

No wonder Old Red Addie had been acting so strange. She'd lost one of her little red-haired family and, like Little Bo Peep and her lost sheep, didn't know where to find it. It would never come home, wagging its pretty curly tail behind it. It would never go to market, never have roast beef, and never go, "Wee-wee-wee" all the way home.

Just then we heard the voice of a running boy, calling from the woods across the road and using the high-pitched tone anybody uses when he is calling a horse.

I unlatched my eyes from the chocolate-colored stains on the ground near the pigpen gate and looked past "Theodore Collins" on our mailbox to the woods across the gravel road. I saw a blue-jeaned, striped-T-shirted boy with flushed face, mussed-up hair, crooked nose, and dragonfly-like eyes spindle-legging his way along the path made by barefoot boys toward the fence and us.

"You guys seen anything of Molly?" he shouted as he came. He kept on running, now yelling up and all around, "Co, Molly! Co, Molly! Where in the world are you?"

Molly, I knew, was their sorrel mare. She was always getting out of their pasture and into other people's pastures or woods or cornfields and was almost as wild as Shorty Long's blue cow—the one you can read about in the story *The Blue Cow.*

Even though Poetry and I had something extra-serious on our minds, Poetry managed to say mischievously, "Leave her alone and she'll come home, bringing her tail behind her."

"She'll bring *two* tails if she does come," Dragonfly panted, stopping and still short of breath from running.

"Two tails?" Poetry squawked back. "Don't be funny!"

"She's going to have a little colt," Dragonfly explained excitedly. "She's run away somewhere so she can have it all by herself. Come on, you guys! Help me find her! I saw her tracks down at the spring, but she wasn't there. She might be along the bayou somewhere!"

I don't know why I said what I said right then. Maybe I shouldn't have, because it almost scared Dragonfly out of what few wits he had. Even though I said it to Poetry and not to Dragonfly, the worried little guy overheard.

What I said was: "Wildcats would rather eat colt meat than any other kind, except deer and little pigs."

Dragonfly's answer was a scared scream. "Wildcats!"

There was no use trying to keep the pop-eyed little guy in the dark about what we knew. So, as fast as we could, we told him about yesterday and last night, showed him the dried blood at Addie's gate, let him count the pigs, and got him as scared as we could before reminding him of what most hunters know— that a wildcat doesn't ever attack a human being unless it's cornered or thinks it is and also thinks it *has* to attack to protect itself.

"But I thought Old Stubtail was in Parke County!" Dragonfly said.

"He was *supposed* to be. Maybe he just has a brother down there," I answered, surprised at what I had thought to say.

The three of us made a quick decision to get going on the search for Molly and get her home and safe in her box stall. Once there, she could celebrate the birth of her baby colt in peace, and there wouldn't be any danger of Old Stubtail's sneaking up on her wherever she was and killing and eating her colt.

As I went into the house to get Betty Lizzie, I was a little bothered about the last part of the eighth commandment for hunting safety. That commandment seemed to be staring at me from the examination paper I'd written out for Dad: "Don't hunt with more than one companion."

But when I told Poetry about it, he said kind of loftyike, "Oh, that's just when they have a gun apiece! Don't you remember? Sometimes the whole gang of us has gone hunting at night with Circus's dad."

I wasn't sure he was right, though, so I ordered both Dragonfly and Poetry to stay behind me as we started toward the spring and the bayou to see if we could find Dragonfly's family's sorrel mare.

At the spring we saw her tracks, but she herself wasn't there.

Up the hill we went, past the leaning linden tree, past the black widow stump, and east along the border of the bayou to the rail fence, on the other side of which is Dragonfly's dad's pasture. I was still in the lead with Betty Lizzie, ready to shoot if I had to.

At the fence a covey of quail exploded out of their hiding place and fanned out into the air in seven or eight different directions, like a giant-sized peacock tail opening. They skimmed over the fence and across a corner of the field and disappeared in good quail cover about a hundred yards up the bayou.

I had Betty Lizzie up and aimed. I almost pulled the trigger but didn't, for I knew I'd just waste a shot. Besides, the season wasn't open for quail, and if I killed one I'd be breaking the law.

I kept Betty Lizzie's safety on all the time, which is part of rule number four, and unloaded her before climbing over the fence to go down into the marshy sedge and brush that bordered the bayou pond.

Over the fence and with Betty Lizzie loaded again, I was careful to keep her muzzle either up or down, always pointed away from all of us, so that if I stumbled over anything and she discharged, the bullet would go off toward the sky or into the ground.

We had no sooner reached the bayou pond and started to skirt it than Dragonfly let out a yell. "There she is! Away over there by the swimming hole! See her! She's all right and safe!"

She was safe, all right, but she wasn't all right—not in her mind. She acted as if she didn't have good horse sense. She was as nervous and trembling as Old Red Addie had been.

Then Dragonfly let out another yell. He broke out from behind me and started a knee-pumping sprint toward the swimming hole and Molly, crying, "Look! She's not fat anymore. She's already had her colt! Let's go see what color it is!"

I swung Betty's muzzle away and quickly unloaded her, because it wasn't safe to have a loaded gun around such an excited boy.

Dragonfly got there ahead of either Poetry or me. "See," he exclaimed proudly, pointing to Molly's colt, lying on its side on the ground. "He's got a white spot on his forehead and one on his rump and . . . and . . ."

Then that spindle-legged, pop-eyed, crooked-nosed little guy let out a bloodcurdling scream, crying, *"He's dead! He's been killed! He's got blood all over him!"*

7

It was one of the saddest sights I'd ever seen. Molly's beautiful brand-new colt, with a long snow-white streak down its forehead all the way from its forelock to the tip of its nose, was lying a few feet from the creek, dead.

I felt myself cringing and scared and wondering. I could see where the teeth of some wild animal had slashed the colt's neck in front of the shoulders and had broken it. And just behind the shoulders there was a bloody place where something had eaten its way in to dig out the heart and liver.

"My colt!" Dragonfly sobbed. "Dad was going to give it to me! What could of done it! What could of!" He broke into wild sobbing that was like a knife jabbing into my heart. Already the bluebottle flies were swarming around the dead colt.

I was holding onto Betty Lizzie, feeling safer just by having her with us. And all the time I was wondering where old Stubtail was by now. What if right that very minute he would break out from behind the shrubbery to get a middle-of-the-morning snack!

It was a shame to have such a beautiful morning spoiled by such dangerous excitement. I was so stirred up inside that the water singing in the riffle below the Sugar Creek swimming hole, the friendly breeze fanning my face, and the juicy notes of the red-winged blackbirds in the trees that bordered the bayou didn't seem wonderful at all, the way they nearly always had other times when I was there.

Dragonfly was so angry and excited and unhappy that I decided to try to cheer him up a little by saying, "We'll put Circus's dad's hounds on his trail again, and this time we'll get him. We'll—"

Dragonfly didn't let me finish. He cut in, his voice trembling and with fire in his eyes, loudly exclaiming, "We'll catch him and kill him and cut *his* heart out!"

It had been a long time since I'd seen Dragonfly so angry. If he hadn't been a Christian, he'd probably have used swear words, which not a one of the gang ever used. It wouldn't be fair to the Person we all tried to live for and whose Name shouldn't be treated as though it was just so much dirt.

I'd maybe better explain right here that it was our Sunday school teacher who had taught us that, saying one morning in class, "Cowards and thoughtless people throw the Name of our Savior around like it was just so much dirt."

It was bad enough having one little red pig stolen and probably eaten. It seemed worse for old Molly to have her only colt killed right in front of her eyes, maybe not more than a few hours after it had been born. It had hardly learned to walk.

Right then is when we heard a dog's voice, a long-toned, bell-like voice that I knew in a flash belonged to Circus's hound pup.

"It's Ichabod!" Dragonfly exclaimed. "He's already found the trail! Come on!" He started off on the run, down the path that led to the bayou, with Poetry and me right after him.

I had Betty Lizzie still unloaded and was wondering how I could obey all the Ten Commandments of Hunting Safety when there were three of us. It'd be almost impossible to keep the fifth commandment, which was never to climb a tree or a fence with a loaded gun. We'd probably have a fence to climb every few minutes. If Ichabod had really found Old Stubtail's trail, he might this time actually stay with it, and we might all of a sudden come upon the colt killer at bay against a rock wall or an outcrop in Old Man Paddler's hills. I might have to shoot quick, or one or the other of us would get killed.

It seemed I *ought* to have the gun loaded. It also seemed I ought not.

I knew what Dad would say if he were there. I also knew what Big Jim, our leader, would order us *not* to do: not let ourselves get into a dangerous hurry but, instead, call Ichabod off the trail and wait for Circus's dad to get back from Parke County with his hounds to organize a hunt with grown-up men.

I kept Betty Lizzie unloaded, so that it would be safe for Poetry and me to run pell-mell after Dragonfly and after Ichabod, whose voice said he was on the other side of the bayou, up in the woods near where we'd flushed the covey of quail.

Pretty soon we were there ourselves. But Ichabod was already gone, galloping in the direction of the leaning linden tree, following the row of evergreens toward the black widow stump. And Dragonfly was still running faster than either Poetry or me.

I yelled for him to stop, but he wouldn't. I was close enough to him to see that he had his Boy Scout knife out and its blade open. That *really* made me worry.

"Stop!" I ordered him in my most savage voice. "Don't ever run with an open-bladed knife! You could fall on it and kill yourself! You could cut your *own* heart out!"

I had warned him too late. All of a sudden, as Dragonfly reached the incline above the spring, he stumbled over something and went down in a topsy-turvy flip-flopping fall. He had been running so fast that falling didn't stop him. He rolled over the lip of the hill and disappeared.

I screamed and ran faster, expecting that when I got there I'd see he had hurt himself with his own knife.

Then, from the direction of the papaw bushes I heard *Circus's* voice scolding loud and hard. "Stop it! Come back here, you mongrel! Leave that rabbit alone!"

I knew Ichabod wasn't any mongrel, which is a dog of mixed breed. Ichabod was a purebred black-and-tan. Circus was calling him a mongrel because he was disgusted with him for some reason.

In an instant, Poetry and I were where Dragonfly had fallen. I certainly felt relieved when I saw he hadn't cut himself in the fall but was only sprawled in a puddle on the other side of the spring reservoir. His hands *and* his face, jeans, and shirt were covered with mud. His knife was lying beside him.

Then I saw Circus. He didn't seem to realize what was going on or that we were anywhere around. He kept on calling Ichabod in a scolding voice. I noticed also that he had picked up a switch and was waiting for his hound to come to him so that he could give him a lesson in hunting—not to get off onto a rabbit trail when he was supposed to be on a red-hot other animal trail.

Just as I thought, Circus gave his cute, very sad little hound a small switching and scolding, saying down to him—and apparently still not realizing that we were around—"Rabbits are *trash!* Do you understand? I started you off on a coon trail, and you were doing fine until that bunny jumped up right in front of your nose, and you let him interrupt you! If you're going to be a trash trailer, you'll be a terrible disappointment. You won't be worth a hill of beans if you don't learn to concentrate!"

I broke in then, saying, "Rabbits aren't trash!" I was thinking how very cute small bunnies are and also remembering one I had seen being eaten by a huge stub-tailed wildcat down by the mouth of the branch yesterday.

"*Part* of the time they're trash," Circus answered like a teacher correcting a boy in class. "Any game the hunter isn't after *at the time* is trash. That's the name they give it. I'm trying to train Ichabod not to get sidetracked onto anything—not rabbit, possum, skunk, or anything—when I've started him on something else."

I looked down at Ichabod's sad face and felt sorry for him. It seemed a shame he'd had to be punished. I guess maybe Circus felt even worse than I did about it, though, for a second later he was down on his knees hugging his cute little black-and-tan and crooning to him, "I've got a plan for your life. I can't let you be a trash trailer. You'll never be any good at trailing wildcats like your mother if you don't learn now! Understand?"

Dragonfly, who was washing his hands and face at the spring, heard what Circus said and called up the incline, "Old Stubtail's come back, and he's killed Molly's new colt and—"

Our spindle-legged little friend came storming up, his open knife in his now-clean right hand, his clothes still mud-spattered, his hair mussed up, and with a set face. "Let's put Ichabod on his trail and chase him down and kill him!"

In only a little while, Circus, Poetry, Dragonfly, Ichabod, and I were back at the swimming hole looking at the dead colt, studying its claw-raked sides. We looked at the place in front of the shoulders where powerful fangs had broken its neck and at the red hole behind the shoulders where the heart and liver had been dug out and eaten.

Circus stood with narrowed eyes, looking down. There was excitement going on in his mind, I could tell. His fists were doubled up, and his jaw muscles were tensing and untensing.

Something exciting was going on in Ichabod's nose too. He hadn't any sooner smelled the colt than he started running in a circle all around us and along the creek bank as though he was trying to find something he had lost or as if his nose was smelling something he'd never smelled before. Whatever it was, it was setting him crazy.

Suddenly that little black-and-tan lifted his long-nosed head and let loose a wild, shrill call with a bell-like tremolo in it like a scared ghost calling for help. Then he took off in a long-legged gallop toward the bayou.

"He's found the trail!" Circus cried. The tone of his voice sent a hunter's thrill chasing up and down my spine.

And then we were all following as fast as we could run.

Across the narrow strip of Dragonfly's dad's cornfield to the bayou and the neck of dry ground between the two long ponds, up the incline to the rail fence and the border of evergreens, the hound went, with the four of us close behind.

At the rail fence the trail swung south along the hedgerow toward Bumblebee Hill and the cemetery at the top. It went through the cemetery and on and on and still on, following the thicket that skirted the rock wall, which, Circus said, was good "cat cover."

And now Ichabod was making a beeline for the Theodore Collins family house. At the elderberry bushes across the road from the walnut tree and our mailbox, the pup began to whimper and act worried as if he had lost the trail. But that was only for a few seconds. In a flash he was over the fence and across the gravel road to our front gate, where he ran from one side to the other to find a place to get over or through.

That's when we heard the sound of a car, and I saw a cloud of dust up the road. It was Dad coming back from Memory City.

Boy oh boy, would we ever have something to tell him! Old Stubtail was back in our territory again and had killed one of our little pigs, had eaten a rabbit at the mouth of the branch, and had killed Molly's new baby colt, and she hadn't even had a chance to celebrate its birth!

I was wondering what kind of a new cousin I had at Memory City, a boy or a girl, and how Wally and his dumb city dog were.

I swung open the gate to let Dad in. Ichabod didn't even bother trying to find out who was coming. Only one thing seemed important to him. He raced through the gate, his nose to the ground, let out another piercing bawl, and shot across the lawn, past the plum tree and the iron pitcher pump, straight for Addie's pen.

Dad swung the car in and stopped in a cloud of dust. The back door of the car was thrust open, and what to my wondering eyes should tumble out but a red-haired, freckled-faced boy my size and an excited copper-colored dog that you already know too much about if you've read the story *The Bull Fighter*.

Dad had brought home with him from Memory City my set-minded, hard-to-get-along-with city cousin, Walford Sensenbrenner, and his uncontrollable dog, Alexander the Copper-smith.

Why on earth had Dad done a thing like that to me and to the Sugar Creek Gang?

What and why and how on earth would we ever manage to live for as long as Alexander the Coppersmith and his master stayed with us?

They certainly had arrived at an exciting time and at a dangerous one too. Just *how* dangerous, none of us knew. Not even Ichabod, who was already out by Addie's gate, running in a worried circle as if he had lost the trail again.

8

Alexander the Coppersmith had come again! In a flurry of fleeting flashes I remembered the wild 10,000 minutes we had had that other summer—especially one exciting, nerve-tingling adventure I'd never be able to forget as long as I lived.

Honestly, that mongrel of a city-bred dog wasn't afraid of the most dangerous danger there ever was! He had even tackled headfirst a snorting, blindly mad, shorthorn bull, actually sinking his sharp teeth into the bull's nose and holding on for dear life. The worried, wild-eyed bull, trying to get Alexander the Coppersmith to let go, had swung around and with a mighty bellow and shake of his head had tossed that copper-colored dog toward the sky.

But that's another story. Right now I have to tell you about a pig-stealing, colt-killing wild-cat, which right that very second Circus's new black-and-tan pup was trailing out near Old Red Addie's gate—one of whose piggies would never again lie in the straw with its mother.

Ichabod seemed to have only one thing on his mind. He didn't even notice Alexander the Coppersmith but was following his snuffling nose all around the gate, where I knew there was chocolate-colored pig's blood and where last night I had seen two green eyes reflecting light from my flashlight and a gray-brown shadow slinking along the garden fence toward the twin pignut trees and the orchard below them.

Right that second, Alexander was standing straight-nosed and stiff-legged, looking toward the gate where Ichabod was worrying his way through a tangle of scents, trying to decide which direction Old Stubtail had gone.

To make things more interesting and noisy, Mixy, who had been lazing on our sloping outside cellar door, woke out of her middle-of-the-morning nap and came as far as the board walk to see what kind of animal had just come plopping out of the car with my city cousin, Wally.

She was probably recalling that other time Alexander had come to our house: the Thanksgiving Day when he had chased her wildly across the barnyard with a turkey tumbling after. Or Mixy might have been remembering fights she had had with different neighborhood dogs.

Anyway, all of a sudden Alexander spied Mixy and started toward her, while she stood stiff-backed and bristling, eyeing him. In a second now, I thought, there would be action.

And there was. A copper-colored city dog made a copper-colored dash at a country cat.

Mixy crouched, flattened her ears, and stood her ground. The second Alexander got to where she was, she thrust out a fierce, fast right front paw with sharp talons on it and slashed and slashed and slashed again, letting loose a jumble of yowls and hisses and wild meows all mixed up with Alexander the Coppersmith's gruff, excited, angry barks and yelps.

The fight was so fierce and so fast that you couldn't tell which animal belonged to the cat family and which to the dog.

Dad, Dragonfly, Circus, Poetry, Wally, and I were in the fight, too—with our voices, that is. Wally was yelling, "Sic 'em!" The rest of us were rooting for Mixy, except for Dad. He was ordering them both to stop.

I was proud of Mixy and the way she stayed right in the middle of that hissing, spitting, yowling, tooth-and-claw, cat and dog fight.

All of a sudden, though, she must have decided she had had enough or had *done* enough to her enemy. As quick as scat, she turned herself into a streak of black and white lightning, shooting across the barnyard to the hole just below the window of the barn, where she would be safe—if she got there first.

She *did* get there first and was safe, and I was again proud that she knew when to quit and run away. She'd live to fight another day.

I expected Wally's mongrel to stay at the small hole into which Mixy had disappeared and bark and bark and bark and pant and try to squeeze himself in after her. But he didn't. Instead, he gave several gruff, disgusted, half-hearted barks in Mixy's direction. Then he swung his copper-colored body around and came trotting back toward the iron pitcher pump where we all were, his tongue hanging out, his sides heaving a little with panting, and with a proud grin on his face that seemed to say, "There! I saved all your lives! I just licked the fur off a savage black and white cat that might have killed all of you! I drove her into a hole under the barn, and she's scared to even stick her nose out!"

The proud expression on his face was the same kind he got when he chased a car down the road.

Just then, from near the pignut trees, Ichabod's dog voice cried, "Come on, you, and help me! While you've been wasting your time on a worthless house cat, I've been untangling the trail of a pig-stealing, colt-killing wildcat! *Woo-o-o-o! Woo-o-o-o!*"

Well, when Circus's cute little hound let loose that long, high-pitched tremolo from the twin pignut trees, it brought all of us to life.

"He's found the trail again!" Circus cried, and away he galloped, past the toolshed and the chicken house on his way to catch up with his excited black-and-tan, which already was halfway to the orchard fence.

Alexander the Coppersmith had come to life even more excited than the rest of us. The second he heard Ichabod's baying, he took one quick stiff-legged, straight-nosed look toward the running hound with an expression on his face that seemed to say that up to now he hadn't even noticed there *was* another dog around. He'd been busy saving our lives.

Then, just as if Ichabod's bawling was a stick somebody had thrown into a creek, expecting him to swim out and bring it back, he was off in a streak of speed to join in the fun or whatever it was that was going on.

"Attaboy!" Wally cried to his mongrel. "Go get him!"

At the orchard fence there was a patch of grass and weeds and wild raspberry bushes that made good cover for quail and that nearly always, in the winter especially, was a shelter for rabbits. There Ichabod ran into trail trouble again. I could tell by the way he was acting that he was trying to decide whether the wildcat had gone through the fence or had followed the fencerow to Poetry's dad's woods in the direction of the mouth of the branch where, yesterday, I'd seen his fierce face for the first time.

Any second now, Alexander the Coppersmith would get to where Ichabod was circling and zigzagging around, trying to find what he had lost, and then what would happen?

I let out a yell for him to stop, to come back, because I knew Alexander didn't have the least idea what a wildcat smelled like or how to follow a cold scent forward or backward. Not knowing how serious things were—a stolen pig, three lambs killed on Harm Groenwald's farm, a brand-new baby colt lying by the swimming hole with its heart and liver eaten out—he'd probably think Ichabod's bawling and strange circlings and zigzaggings were some kind of game that country dogs play.

And then he was there and all over everywhere, getting in Ichabod's way, biting at him playfully and barking as if what few wits he had had turned into a Sugar Creek cyclone.

He was like a car that didn't have good brakes. In a fast charge at Ichabod, he whammed into his shoulder with his own shoulder and bowled him over. The two of them landed *scratchety-sizzle* in a tangled-up scramble in the raspberry bushes. And that's when Ichabod's voice changed into a series of short, sharp, more-than-ever-excited barks. For a second I thought he had lost his temper and that there was going to be a fierce dogfight there in the bushes.

But I was wrong. Instead, a brown flash of bunny shot out into the open and raced hippety-hop down the fence row toward Poetry's dad's woods. Ichabod and Alexander both gave chase with a bedlam of dog voices, which was enough to scare the poor rabbit even worse than Peter Rabbit had been scared in the story where Mr. McGregor was after him with a garden rake.

Seeing the rabbit flying in long leaps ahead of the also-flying, barking dogs, Circus let out a yell. "Hey, Ichabod! Stop! That's a *rabbit!* Come back here!"

To the rest of us he complained, "He's going to be hard to teach! I'll have to give him another switching!"

With that he stooped, quickly picked up a branch Dad had pruned from the peach tree by the fence, and was off on a fast run toward the fence way down at the end of our pasture.

By now both dogs were running excitedly back and forth, trying to find a place where they could get through the fence. The smart bunny had already squeezed through and was safe somewhere in Poetry's dad's woods.

Finally, both dogs heard Circus's angry voice, and both dogs started back toward where we were.

I felt sorry for little Ichabod, because the history of my own life had some switchings mixed up in it. And if there is anything that hurts me worse than getting a switching myself, it's to see somebody's pet switched or even scolded—a hound especially, because he always acts so sad and crouches low and looks up at you with every wrinkle on his long face seeming to say, "Please, Mister. I'm sorry. I didn't know it was wrong to do it. Please."

The closer Ichabod got to Circus, the sadder he looked. By the time he was within ten feet, he was actually crawling. Then he stopped and looked up with sad brown eyes, every movement saying, "I'm sorry . . . please . . ."

I took one look at Circus's set face and knew he was thinking hard and wishing he didn't have to do what I also knew he had to do. Nobody could train a hound not to chase rabbits or get sidetracked, unless the hound knew for sure his master wouldn't stand for it.

I hadn't known that Little Jim, the littlest member of the gang, was anywhere around until all of a sudden from behind us I heard his tearful voice almost screaming, "Don't! Don't, Circus. Don't! He doesn't know any better. He—"

"That's why I'm punishing him," Circus called back grimly, "so he *will* know."

Then Circus said something I didn't understand at the time but which later I did. He looked around at all of us with kind of sad eyes himself. "I'm giving him a licking not to punish him for being *bad* but to make him a good trailer. I have a good plan for him, and I have to help him find out what it is."

The switching Circus gave his cute little black-and-tan hound pup was about the easiest switching a dog ever got. With one hand he held onto Ichabod's collar, and with the other he swung the switch . . . one . . . two . . . three . . . four. Circus actually switched Ichabod harder with his *voice*, saying crossly, "Rabbits are out! Do you understand? Out! When you're on a coon or a fox or a wildcat trail, you're not to let yourself get sidetracked! Understand?"

Then all of a sudden Circus flung his switch to the ground, dropped to his knees, pressed his cheek against his hound's head, hugged him close, and begged, "I'm sorry, pal! Please don't hate me for it! But I had to do it, even if it *was* bad company that got you started. Bad company, do you hear? Don't ever let any other dog lead you astray!" Circus glared angrily at a fidgety Alexander the Coppersmith, not more than ten feet away.

Wally overheard that and exclaimed, "Don't

you dare call my dog bad company! He's a good dog!"

You never saw a dog change his attitude so quickly. All in a second, Ichabod was happy again, nuzzling his face up to Circus's and wagging his long tail. It seemed the dog was trying to say to Circus, "Don't feel bad. I'll forgive you . . ." And I noticed there were tears in Circus's eyes as there had been in his voice when he had apologized to Ichabod.

I couldn't help thinking about Alexander, wondering if anybody had a good plan for *his* life and if his life would ever be worth anything. I'd tried so hard to teach him a few dog manners the other time Wally had come to spend 10,000 minutes at our house.

There certainly was a difference in the way those two canines were getting trained and also in the way they came back from chasing the rabbit. Ichabod had returned to his master with a sad face, acting sorry for what he had done wrong, whatever it was. Wally's mongrel had raced back proudly, his long tongue hanging out, a grin on his whiskered face as if to say, "There! I chased *another* wild animal away, clear down to the woods. I've saved all your lives again!"

Wally, seeing what Circus had done, must have thought he ought to give Alex a little training, too. He picked up the switch Circus had tossed away and started after his dog, scolding and saying, "Come here, you rascal! Rabbits are out! Understand? Out!"

But there wasn't any change in the attitude of Alexander the Coppersmith. Instead of coming humbly to his master to find out what he'd done that he shouldn't have, he stood stiff-legged and straight-nosed, gave two or three short gruff, disgusted barks, tossed his head, whirled all the way around, and ran off toward the pignut trees. There he stopped and looked back.

"Come here, you rabbit chaser!" Wally yelled crossly and with the switch in his hand started on the run toward him.

It was a very interesting sight to watch— Alexander the Coppersmith standing stiffly, looking down the incline at us, his beady eyes on Wally and the switch, and Wally, red-haired and freckled and flush-faced, hurrying toward him, shouting, "Don't you dare run away! Do you hear me? Don't you dare!"

But his mongrel dared. He wheeled about, looked in our direction again, and bounded away with Wally right after him.

"Wait!" Circus called to Wally. "I'll get him for you." He quickly stooped and picked up an old stick. Then he yelled a cheerful yell toward the pignut trees and tossed the two-foot-long stick as far as he could in the direction of the orchard fence where the raspberry bushes were, calling at the same time, "Go get it!"

That was a game Alex understood. We'd played it with him many a time the week he'd spent here last year. Every time we tossed a stick anywhere, even out into the water, he'd race after it, catch it up in his happy mouth, and come flying back to us.

Now there was a copper streak of dog shooting across the stretch of pasture, and in seconds Alex was back where we were, holding the stick in his mouth.

"Don't you touch him with that switch!" Circus ordered Wally. "It's been too long since he chased the rabbit. He wouldn't understand anything you'd do to him now. Besides you might *want* him to chase rabbits. A good rabbit dog is worth money."

And that was that.

Dad called then from the gate near Addie's pig house. "You boys seen anything of a missing pig? One of the baby pigs is missing!"

I'd almost forgotten Dad. My mind had been tangled up with everything else.

In a little while we were where he was, showing him the chocolate-colored dried blood. We told him about Dragonfly's dead colt down by the swimming hole, the savage wildcat I'd seen eating a bunny yesterday when I'd been fishing at the mouth of the branch, and the excitement of last night at the chicken house.

I could see Dad's jaw muscles tensing and knew he was getting stirred up inside. We were really in a situation. Circus's dad was gone to Parke County with his hounds to help the farmers over there catch a sheep-killing predator, and all of a sudden we find that Old Stubtail is back in our own territory again, killing right and left. Something would have to be done.

We'd have to get a phone call through to Dan Browne as quick as we could and get him back here with the dogs.

Dad got his thoughts interrupted right then by the sound of a long, high-pitched tremolo from down near the raspberry bushes. It was Ichabod again. He was zigzagging around where he and Alexander the Coppersmith had had their tangled-up scramble and where the rabbit had its nest and out of which it had exploded like a rocket and gone hippety-hop down the fencerow.

Ichabod was making such a noisy noise and seemed so extra excited that I guessed he had found Old Stubtail's trail again and was untangling it.

Wally had a different idea. As soon as he heard Ichabod's baying, he said to Circus, "Lot of good it did to give him a lickin'! There he goes again after another rabbit."

But there Ichabod *didn't* go—not on another rabbit trail, anyway. He whisked through an opening in the fence and was off at a gallop right down through the center of the orchard, his nose to the ground every few feet, his musical tremolo singing out on the warm, sunshiny air every few seconds.

"Come on!" different ones of us yelled to the rest of us. "Let's follow him!"

Dad stopped all of us with his gruff voice, ordering, "Wait, boys. A wildcat would tear your hound to shreds if he brought him to bay. Call off your dog, Circus!"

Circus had a different idea. "But the trail's hot! It's fresh! The time to chase him to his den is *now!* It might be a week before we'll run onto another hot track like this one."

Well, Dad wasn't used to having a boy anywhere near my age talk back to him, so he used a *very* strong dadlike voice when he ordered Circus, "Call him off! You don't want your hound killed! I'll go in and get your father on the phone right away and tell him Old Stubtail's back here and to come on home fast."

I could see Circus didn't *want* to obey some other boy's father. Still, he did try to by calling Ichabod and whistling for him.

But Ichabod also had a different idea. Already he was far down at the other end of the orchard. I could see him at the woven wire fence down there, squeezing through into Poetry's dad's woods.

"We've got to stop him!" Circus said grimly.

I could tell from the expression on his face that he believed my dad. It'd never do to let an innocent hound pup get into a fang-fight with a wildcat. Ichabod would be torn to pieces. The teeth I'd seen on Old Stubtail yesterday were big enough, sharp enough, and strong enough to bite right through the head of a dog the size of Ichabod.

All of us except Alexander the Coppersmith started on the run after Circus to try to help him stop his hound from getting killed. The only reason Alexander didn't start was that already he was down where Ichabod was, running wild all around in front of and behind and in the way of him, as if he was trying to get attention. Or maybe he wanted to make us think it was his own nose that was doing all the trailing. I knew that excitable city dog didn't have the least idea what was going on.

What I didn't know was that, in less than a half hour, Alexander the Coppersmith was going to see his first wildcat and find out that chasing a black and white house cat into a hole under a barn was a lot different from suddenly happening upon a twenty-eight toothed, sharp-taloned, savage-tempered *really* wild wildcat.

9

I chabod turned out to be one of the fastest trailers that ever trailed a trail. He was also, I thought, one of the most stubborn hound pups I ever saw or heard.

In my mind, while we were running pell-mell after him and Alexander the Copper-smith, I had one main purpose—to stop Ichabod from all of a sudden catching up with Old Stubtail and getting his eyes scratched out.

One thing I didn't notice at first was that with all the yelling Circus was doing, ordering his pup to stop, he wasn't using a scolding voice.

He was yelling, "Stop! Leave that wildcat alone! You'll get your ears slit to ribbons! You're no good as a catch dog! You're only a trailer!" But he wasn't using a tone of voice like the tone he had used several times that morning when he'd been disgusted with Ichy for trailing trash.

It sounded more as if Dan Browne's son was whooping it up at a basketball game, rooting for his team to win. It was as if he was urging his cute little black-and-tan purebred hound to stay on the job. To keep on keeping on. To chase Old Stubtail to his lair or actually catch up with him and get into a fierce fang-fight.

When we reached the mouth of the branch

where I'd first seen Old Stubtail eating a rabbit and where I'd had the dream of wildcats riding up and down a golden escalator, I panted to Circus, "How come he won't obey you? How come he keeps right on?"

Circus leaped across a narrow place in the stream, landed on the other side, and answered me. "He's not trailing trash! If I'd scold him now, he might think we didn't *want* him to trail wildcats! He'd think I think he was trailing trash, and he might be spoiled! I gotta let him do it!"

"But my father ordered you to stop him!" I protested.

Wally and the rest of the gang were quite a distance behind us, and only I heard what Circus answered. "*My* father would want me to whoop it up for Ichabod! He'd let him learn to trail. Then right at the last minute, if there was any danger, he'd use a different tone of voice. He'd stop him from *catching* but not from *trailing!*"

And that was that.

I knew that Dad was back at the house trying to put through a long-distance call to Mr. Browne in Parke County somewhere. And here we were, already a half mile from home, and he wasn't here to order his own son to stop. Dad hadn't noticed that I had Betty Lizzie with me, either, and of course he hadn't ordered me not to take her.

Now that the chase was on, I thought, we might run into an emergency that'd mean I either had to use Betty Lizzie or one or the other of six boys and two dogs might get killed.

Pound . . . pound . . . pound . . . pound. My heart was beating hard, and it wasn't just from running.

All of a sudden from behind me I heard Little Jim's excited voice exclaim, "Everybody! Look! Out there in the creek!"

I looked, and there, straight out from the willow where I'd tied my whopper of a bass on the stringer, was a V-shaped water trail moving parallel with the shore. The small brown head of some wild animal was at the point of it.

A glad feeling shot through me. *There* was proof that I had had a fish on the stringer. I didn't answer Little Jim, but I did yell to Poetry, "There, smarty. There's what ate my whopper of a bass!"

Poetry was closer than I'd thought, and his answer was so loud in my ears it almost deafened me. "Right, smarty! I knew it all the time. I saw that muskrat yesterday while I was up on the tree trunk."

On and on and still on we went. At the cave, Ichabod, with Alexander running circles all around him and acting as if he was enjoying this new country dog game, didn't even bother to take one tiny sniff. He zigzagged right on, following the path into the swamp, just the way Jay and Bawler had done quite a few other times when they'd been on Old Stubtail's trail. Boy oh boy oh boy!

"He's headed for Old Man Paddler's hills

again!" Dragonfly's raspy voice cried from behind all of us. He was short of breath on account of his hay fever and a little asthma.

I still wasn't quite sure I was doing right, but it seemed I was. I knew my father wanted Circus to call off his dog, and he would also expect his son to help Circus do it. Yet, my same father was always happy when the gang was together having what he and Mom called "wholesome fun," if we weren't supposed to be doing something else at the time. The only thing was, he *didn't* know that while Dan Browne's son was ordering his dog to stop, he was using a tone of voice that was like saying, "Attaboy, Ichabod! Keep on doing what you're doing. You're doing a great job. Go to it! You're a super dog. Wonderful!"

We had to slow down in the swamp because Ichabod was having nose trouble. It seemed he was not able to untangle the wildcat's smart, mixed-up trail.

In a few minutes now we'd get to the middle of the swamp, where the water, backing into it from Sugar Creek, had made a big pond. I was remembering another time when Wally and Alexander had been here with us. Wally had kept his nervous quadruped on a leash then. We hadn't wanted to run the risk of his running wild all over everywhere. He might accidentally get out into the quagmire, sink down, and never come back up.

The pond was such an exciting place. Marsh hens were swimming along, leaving nervous V-shaped water trails behind them. Turtles that had been sunning themselves on a log plopped off into the water all of a sudden. Dragonflies were sailing around all over, while red-winged blackbirds furnished music. The whole area was a happy place to be, a place to feel lazy in. The grassy hillock on the shore begged a drowsy boy to take an afternoon nap.

Ichabod wasn't bothered by marsh hens swimming, redwings singing, turtles splashing, or anything else. He was on a trail of something that wasn't trash. His master was whooping it up for him to keep on keeping on. So he kept on.

It was different with Alexander the Coppersmith. When we got to the edge of the pond, he stopped and stood stiff-legged and straight-nosed, looking in the direction of the middle of the swamp as if he was using his mind for something that wasn't play. If he was thinking, I knew what was bothering him. It was the memory of that other time we'd brought him through here and he'd had a fierce underwater fight with a snapping turtle.

I looked to see what was worrying him, and, sure enough, there was the giant turtle, his nose and heavy-lidded eyes looking like drops of transparent blood sticking up above the surface of the water. I got a glimpse of the rest of him under the water just as I had the last time I'd seen him. He was even bigger than he'd been then, having had time to grow some more.

This time Alexander wasn't interested in

getting out into the water to see what was there.

Dragonfly maybe remembered the time somebody had thrown a stick out into the water and Alex had plunged in after it. Anyway, right that second he tossed a piece of driftwood out toward the snapper's nose.

Alexander might not have had good sense most of the time, but he did know enough to know that it is better to use your head than it is to get it snapped off by a giant-sized snapper. Or as my dad says, "It's better to have good sense than it is to be brave."

Anyway, Alex let out a whimper and made a dive for Wally, who, the second he got to him, quick grabbed his collar and snapped on his leash.

Well, it wasn't the time to enjoy our favorite nature's paradise. Certainly not right then. From what seemed maybe two hundred yards ahead there came Ichabod's high-pitched, musical wail. He'd untangled Stubtail's trail and was running in full cry in the direction of the rocky hills above Old Man Paddler's cabin.

Circus let out a thrilling yell, crying, "He's headed for the haunted house! I'll bet Old Stubtail's got his den in the attic where the mother coon used to live!"

And the chase was on again.

What would happen this time? Would it be like all the other times when Dan Browne's hounds had run on Stubtail's red-hot trail, up and down the hills, across dry canyons, in and out of brier thickets, along the edges of out-crops and high ledges with jagged rocks below, and then finally had lost the scent and couldn't find it again? I wished with my whole heart it'd be different this time.

We'd no sooner reached the clearing on the other side of the swamp than Wally's dog changed from a scaredy-cat to an excited wild-running, impossible-to-manage mongrel again.

"Oh, no, you don't," Wally cried, holding onto his leash with all his strength. "You're not going to run wild up there in those rocks! You don't watch your footing! You'd make a dash for a rabbit or a bird or leap across a gully and miss the other side, and down you'd go. Stop!" He screamed his order toward the animal on the other end of his leash.

The second he said it, I saw a flash of black and tan away up on a ledge above a lot of out-crops. Circus's hound pup stopped stock-still in his tracks and was looking back down at his master.

Circus fired up at that and barked to Wally. "Don't you *dare* yell like that again! Ichy thought it was *me* ordering him to stop. We've got to let him go, let him do what we want him to!"

"I was yelling at *my* dog!" Wally defended himself. His tone of voice was so surly that I knew if things hadn't been the way they were, there might have been a fistfight.

Just that second Little Jim let out a yell from away up ahead of us. I was so astonished I almost jumped out of my tracks. I'd supposed he was *behind* us.

I looked in the direction his high-pitched, cheerful yell had come from, and there he was, standing high on the dead trunk of a fallen tree. When the tree had gone down, one end had landed on the other side of the narrow gulch.

"Look what yesterday's storm did!" he cried down to us. "It made a bridge for us to go across on!"

Little Jim was right. The big ponderosa pine that had stood so many years all alone on the edge of the gulch had blown over. And there, right out in the middle of the tree bridge, stood Little Jim, holding onto one of the upright branches.

In my mind's eye I was seeing Little Jim's acrobatic actions of the past several weeks: "skinning the cat" on the two-by-four of our grape arbor, balancing himself as he walked across the high beam in our haymow, jumping off into the hay, turning a half somersault in the air and landing on his back in the soft hay, learning to do the cartwheel like Circus, our acrobat, who could do it almost as well as the clown at the Sugar Creek county fair.

What, I thought, cringing, *if that little rascal, away out there on that tree trunk bridge over a gully with jagged rocks in it, should decide all of a sudden he wanted to do some kind of a stunt for us to watch?*

What if he was imagining himself to be a stuntman and the rest of us an imaginary crowd of thousands of cheering people?

If you're a boy or have ever known anybody who couldn't help it because he was one, you can maybe guess that another thought was in my mind right then. It was this: I, Bill Collins, Theodore Collins's only son, would himself like to climb up to where the tree bridge was and work my way across to the wide ledge on the other side!

That ledge was the one place in all the Sugar Creek territory I had never been. We had never found any way for us to get there except by going around behind Old Man Paddler's cabin, up and up and up, and then letting ourselves down on a rope. We had talked about doing that but had decided it was too dangerous and too dumb for a boy to do.

But if Little Jim should lose his balance or accidentally let go of the upright branch he was holding onto, I thought, what would happen? There wasn't any net for him to fall into such as the acrobat at the fair had had. There were only rocks and—

The thought had to be shut out of my mind, and nobody ought to put it into Little Jim's mind either, or he might get scared, lose his balance, fall, and . . . and . . .

Using as calm a voice as I could, I called up to him to be careful, to come back across to our side, and to wait till we could come up and examine the bridge to see if it was safe to try to cross on. If only I could get him to come back before he went any farther . . .

Several of the others called to him, too.

Alexander the Coppersmith was straining and whimpering at the end of his leash, wanting to get to wherever Ichabod was, somewhere up ahead of us.

Just that second, Ichabod let out a fresh, wailing tremolo. It sounded now as if he had worked his way across the canyon and was on the other side somewhere, not far from the place where his mother and her big, rangy, hunting dog companion had always lost the trail before.

Our voices warning Little Jim to wait for us before going across were like Circus's orders to Ichabod for him to stop. They only spurred him on. He called back to us, "Who's afraid of the big bad wolf?"

Wally called up to him then and said, "It's a wildcat we're after, not a wolf," which was an unnecessary remark, I thought.

Anyway, it didn't help any. Little Jim carefully worked his way across the tree trunk bridge, and before long there he was on the other side, waving to us and calling, "Come on up and over! Come on in—the water's fine!" That's nearly always what the first one in the old swimming hole yells back to the rest of us.

Another voice sounded then. Ichabod's dog voice all of a sudden broke out into an excited series of bawls, barks, yelps, and chops that said he was getting close to his quarry and for us all to come and help him or else *watch* him make short work of a fierce-fanged wildcat.

Then a flash of black and tan appeared

about a hundred yards beyond Little Jim. Ichabod had found a way for a dog to get onto that long, wide ledge! Now the hound was working his way around the base of a gnarled, weather-killed, twisted juniper, whose roots were somewhere below in the side of the cliff.

I cringed as I watched Ichabod zigzag here and there, sniffing at the face of the cliff to see if Old Stubtail had gone up. He acted as if there was so much wildcat smell on the ledge that it was as hard for him to find the trail as it would be for a boy to work his way blindfolded through a brier patch. Every second, though, he was getting nearer to Little Jim.

At one narrow place on the ledge where there was another juniper, I saw a bird fly from a nest and go scooting along the ledge for several feet before taking wing out across the sky. For a few seconds Ichabod stopped, stood with nose pointed at it, then dropped his head to the rocky ledge as much as to say, "That is trash! My master wants me to stick to my job!"

And then he was busy again, snuffling his way toward where Little Jim stood proudly near the top end of the tree trunk bridge. Little Jim was pleased with himself for not being afraid and was maybe imagining himself to be a clown high in a big outdoor tent doing acrobatic stunts.

It was then that, like a streak of lightning going through my mind, I saw a flash of gray-brown animal between Little Jim and Ichabod. The animal was backed up against the cliff, his ears flattened, ready to fight anything or anybody, tooth and talon and fang.

At almost the same second I saw him, Ichabod changed his tone and began barking "treed." That little untrained, unafraid dog-child of Bawler had succeeded where his mother, one of the best hunting hounds in the country, and old Jay had failed a half-dozen times. He'd trailed a colt-killing, pig-stealing, sheep-killing marauder to his lair.

I say *lair* because that's where Old Stubtail was. Under an overhanging rock was his den, a deep depression in the cliff wall going back in maybe four feet.

The only way for the wildcat to get away from Ichabod now would be to go farther the other way, and the "other way" was toward where Little Jim was. I also noticed that there was only ten more feet of ledge for Little Jim to retreat to, if he had to. Just those ten feet behind him was the *end* of the ledge. It stopped at a rock wall that went straight up.

Any second now, Ichabod would be close enough for Stubtail to thrust out a long, talon-filled paw and rake in that purebred pup. Then he would either tear him to pieces or open his jaws and just bite through his head. And that'd be the last of one of the finest little dogs there ever was.

For the first time, Little Jim seemed to realize what danger he was in. He realized it because all of us were yelling to him to get to the tree trunk bridge and come back.

But now the big cat was closer to the tree trunk than he was. In fact, the den in the wall was almost at the very end of the treetop.

In a minute now, Ichabod would be there from the other side of the cat. There'd be a savage half-minute fight, and it'd be all over for Ichabod. And then what would happen to Little Jim?

Something had to be done. But I knew, and I guess Wally and Circus and Poetry realized the same thing, that not one of us could get there in time to help Little Jim.

I loaded Betty Lizzie and started toward the fallen ponderosa trunk. But how could I shoot when Ichabod was leaping in and out, snapping at Old Stubtail? And Little Jim was in my line of fire, too!

In my hurry and because of the cyclone in my mind, I quickly stooped, picked up a three-foot-long club from a dead tree, whirled, and threw it as hard as I could straight for the cliff wall near Little Jim. "Use this to fight with if you have to!" I yelled across to him.

Then Ichabod was there, and the fight was on. Circus was screaming for him to stop, but Ichabod didn't realize he was supposed to be only a trailer and not a catch dog. He was in the fight tooth and toenail. So far he was being missed by all the wildcat's savage thrusts with his claws.

Little Jim saw the club strike the wall, bounce back, and fall not more than six feet from the fight. He made a dive for it.

Then, I guess Old Stubtail thought he was being attacked from two sides, that he had to fight not only a dog but a human being as well.

He turned from Ichabod and snarled at Little Jim, his fangs bared. In another minute, I expected to see Little Jim get killed.

I couldn't stand to look, but I also couldn't look away.

But now something else was going on. With all the excitement on the other side of the gully, a city-bred mongrel of a dog that wasn't afraid of anything except a snapping turtle and that had been trained to chase after every stick anybody threw anywhere—that city dog had come to wild life at the end of Wally's leash.

Alexander had always wanted to be in the middle of whatever excitement there was. Now he reared, plunged, and pulled savagely. And suddenly, like a covey of quail being flushed, he was gone, and only a leash with an empty dog collar on it was left in Wally's hand.

A copper-colored streak with four flying legs on it was on its way to the tree trunk bridge, out on it, and across. With a rush of flying teeth and legs and barks, he charged head-first toward the wildcat fight.

He'd chased a dangerous black-and-white house cat under a barn. He'd driven a wild cottontail down a hedgerow to Poetry's dad's woods. Now he was on the way to save all of us and Ichabod and Little Jim from an insignificant wildcat that he could lick with one tooth.

Before you could have said "Jack Robinson

Crusoe," Alexander the Coppersmith was there. He was there head-and-teeth-first, and he didn't get stopped by flying cat claws. He rushed in, getting there while Little Jim was still standing, club raised, prepared to meet Old Stubtail's flying tackle if he sprang toward the cutest little guy that was ever a member of the Sugar Creek Gang.

In another second—or even a half second—that'd have been the end of Little Jim.

But *then* was when Alexander the Coppersmith struck. His whole body slammed into the wildcat. There was so much fast and noisy action for a few seconds that you couldn't even see what was happening.

I knew only one thing, and that was that Alexander the Coppersmith, the city-bred dog that couldn't be managed and wouldn't obey orders, had landed right in the center of a new kind of dog game.

It was all over before we scarcely realized it had started. The cat and Alexander the Coppersmith, scratching and biting and rolling and hissing, got too near the rim of the ledge, and over they went together, *down . . . down . . . down . . .*

DOWN!

I heard their bodies crash on the rocks below and saw them bounce off a jutting rock and go hurtling to the bottom of the canyon.

10

It took us quite a while to work our way down the canyon wall to the bottom where Old Stubtail and Alexander were, and it was hard to believe what we found when we did get there.

Wally, sobbing and holding his empty leash, reached the scene first. The rest of us got there only a few seconds later. We'd waited for Little Jim to come back across the tree trunk bridge before we started down.

All the way down I kept thinking of what had happened on the ledge, the whole exciting, dangerous thing. I remembered Stubtail, with his back to the den in the canyon wall, his ears flattened in anger, his body crouching, ready to spring at Ichabod. Then he realized Little Jim was not more than five feet from him with a club in his hand. Maybe deciding in a flash that Little Jim was going to try to kill him, he was ready to leap straight for that little guy.

Then, what had made the excitement even more like a tornado was a copper-colored city dog, who didn't know what danger was, streaking across the tree trunk bridge and crashing head-on with the wildcat. He met Old Stubtail in midair. And Little Jim's life had been saved.

It was one of the saddest sights we'd ever seen. It just didn't seem possible, but it was the truth, and we had to believe it. Not more than two feet apart, on a pile of jagged rocks, were the broken and bloody bodies of the stub-tailed, fierce-fanged colt-killer and a reckless, uncontrollable, city-bred mongrel.

Little Jim, with tears in his eyes, stood with the rest of us in a little semicircle. He was the first one to say anything, and he broke into sobs as he said, "He saved my life! He got there just in time!"

I guess we were all about as sad as we ever had been, on account of Alexander the Coppersmith's getting killed in his fall on the rocks. But we were glad that Little Jim was alive and with us.

For just a second I had a flash of thought about a golden stairway leading up and up and up. It seemed that maybe an angel had come swooping down, and *that* was the reason Little Jim had been saved. Anyway, he *was* spared, and I knew who had spared him, even if He had used a dog to do it. It felt fine to believe that.

Wally said something then, bringing my thoughts back to our sad circle. I guess I had forgotten that, the last time he had come to visit us, we had made him an honorary member of the gang and that also he had decided to become a Christian. But when he said what he said the *way* he said it, so reverently and with tears in his voice—and also while he was on his knees trying to hug his dead dog—I all of a sudden went blind with my own tears. I never will forget what he said as long as I live.

"Old pal, I guess God had a plan for your life, too!" Then he broke into crying as people sometimes do at a funeral.

So I didn't get a chance to use Betty Lizzie on Old Stubtail, because he was already dead. One thing we all noticed was that there was a jagged, bloody place on his throat, as if some animal had sunk its teeth into him. We knew *what* animal had done it when, a few seconds later, we saw Wally picking little tufts of wildcat fur from Alexander's teeth.

At first we thought we'd try to get Alexander's body home and, as Little Jim suggested, "bury him under the papaw bushes and put up a tombstone, and every year on Memorial Day put flowers there, and—"

But Wally said, cutting in on him, "No, we'll bury him right here. Right where he fell in battle."

Wally had a right to decide it, since he was the nearest relative. Besides, when I looked up the steep canyon wall and thought about the long trip through the swamp and how heavy Alexander was, I thought the pallbearers would have a very hard time of it.

I took off my hat in a hurry and used it to shoo away several bluebottle flies that had come from somewhere and were buzzing about the two corpses at our feet. That was another reason that we ought to have the funeral right away.

"How come you want to bury him *here?*" Dragonfly wanted to know.

Wally answered, "Don't they have a cemetery at Gettysburg where the Battle of Gettysburg was fought?"

Poetry, being good in history, said they did. "They dedicated it on November 19, 1863. That's when Abraham Lincoln made his famous Gettysburg address."

First, we dragged Old Stubtail back a ways. Then, with our bare hands and with sticks and sharp rocks, we scooped out a place for Alexander's grave. It was pretty hard and stony soil to dig in, and so that it wouldn't be too shallow a grave, we piled rocks and rocks and more rocks on top.

We stepped back to look at it, not a one of us saying anything but all of us gulping a little. Then we faced east the way people did on Armistice Day in respect for the dead, took off our hats, and stood with our heads bowed a minute or so. And the funeral was over.

Even though the wildcat was heavier than Alexander, we decided to try to take him home. Getting him to the top of the canyon wall was the hardest part.

Ichabod was acting very happy, but the gang wasn't. Ordinarily we'd have felt proud of ourselves, Circus especially, because it was his own dog that had done a better job of trailing than Ichabod's experienced mother—better, even, than old Jay, one of the best-known "cat" catchers in the whole county.

When we got back to the place where the ponderosa had fallen, Circus stopped us and surprised us by saying, "You guys stay here a minute. I want to go back across and see if I can find her cubs!"

"*Her cubs!*" different ones of us yelped back at him.

"Yes," Circus answered grimly. "Her cubs. Old Stubtail was a mother!"

Circus was right. Stubtail *was* a mother. Her body showed that she'd been nursing her babies.

Wally spoke up then and said, "I want one of them for a pet."

I remembered that last year he'd wanted a pet *polecat* and had actually taken a descented one home with him to Memory City!

Well, I'll have to stop writing in just a few minutes, because the adventure we had when we came back and took the two cute little kitten wildcats alive is another story, which, added onto this one, would make it too long.

For some reason, though, when I found out about there being two wildcat babies left motherless and thought how their mother—who was what is called "carnivorous," so *had* to have raw flesh to eat because that was the way she was made—well, it was hard to be glad she was dead.

I *could* be glad that she wouldn't steal any more of Old Red Addie's curly tailed pigs or any of Harm Groenwald's lambs or anybody's baby colts. And I was thankful that Little Jim's life had been saved.

Poetry explained it to Wally and me a little later that day when we were over at his house, waiting for dinner to be ready. We were in his tent in their backyard at the time.

He was showing us his shell collection. "See all these empty shells?" he asked Wally and me.

"They certainly are pretty," Wally answered. He had one of Poetry's dull white, two-and-a-half-inch-long Iceland cockles in his hand, admiring it, and I could see that maybe he'd want to start a hobby of collecting shells himself sometime.

But Poetry had something special on his mind. I thought so from the way he was wrinkling his forehead. I knew for sure when he said, "Once there was a bivalve mollusk living in this little shell house. But it died and left its shell behind. Everything in nature has to die sometime."

I heard Wally gulp. I knew he was thinking about a pile of stones up in Old Man Paddler's rocky hills, where, at the bottom of a ravine, Alexander the Coppersmith lay buried. It wasn't pleasant to think what we were all thinking right then, but we couldn't help it.

I was glad when we were interrupted by a high-pitched tremolo from the direction of the back door. It was Poetry's mother wanting us to come to dinner.

That night when I was upstairs in my room getting ready to go to bed, I stood for a few minutes looking out at the moonlit backyard, past the chicken house and Addie's apartment. Wally was in the other room in his own bed, sound asleep. I could tell by the snoring, which I remembered from last year.

It had been an exciting day. My mind certainly had a lot of things to think about. It seemed I was a whole lot older than I had been this time last night—years and years and years. So much had happened. I'd learned a lot of different things. Then, as my parents had taught me to do, I knelt beside my bed to make a good-night prayer to the heavenly Father and to ask Him about anything that might be on my mind.

I was surprised when I heard myself whispering to Him, "Please help Bill Collins not to be a trash trailer in life. Help me to find out for sure what You want me to be and to stay on the track without getting off on anything You *don't* want me to do. Help me to do only what is right . . ."

I can't remember finishing my prayer or getting into bed. But I *must* have finished it, and I *must* have crawled in between Mom's nice clean sheets, because only a few minutes later (or so it seemed), I was wide awake in bed, the sun was shining outside, and I could hear birds singing in the woods across the road.

Moody Press, a ministry of the Moody Bible Institute, is designed for education, evangelization, and edification.
If we may assist you in knowing more about Christ and the Christian life, please write us without obligation:
Moody Press, c/o MLM, Chicago, Illinois 60610.